Written
in the Stars

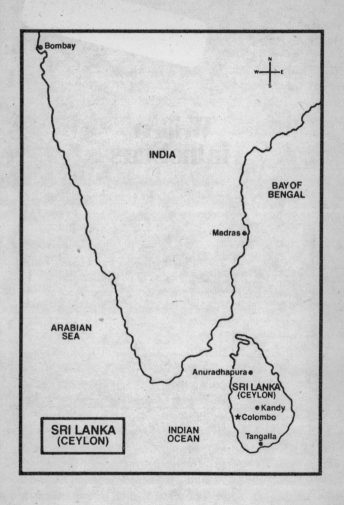

Chapter One

The drums sounded like thunder, reverberating around the illuminated temple and the surrounding hills. There were the temple drums, the martial drums of past armies, and the festive drums of the dance. Some were struck by the hands alone, some with padded and unpadded sticks, some with one hand and a drum-stick in the other hand. Each drummer was intent on his own complicated rhythm, many of them created especially for the occasion, and the whole merged into a mighty, deafening roar that electrified the body and stunned the mind.

Miranda Wade took up her stance against the wall of the Dalada Maligawa which houses one of the most sacred relics of the Buddhist world, the sacred Tooth of the Lord Buddha himself, rescued from his funeral pyre some six hundred years before the birth of Christ.

It had been a lucky chance which had brought

Miranda to Kandy in Sri Lanka at this particular time of the year. She had never heard of the famous procession which takes place in the lunar month of Esala in July or August for ten nights and a day in a festival of dance and pageantry that has to be seen to be believed. Miranda was a fashion photographer, but this was too good a chance to be missed and she had brought her cameras with her to make the most of the scene that encompassed the whole gem of a city, was reflected in the lake that stood at its feet, and was brought to life by a whole people intent on paying their respect to the Sacred Relic.

None of Miranda's companions had wanted to come with her. One of the girls who had been engaged to model the collection against the romantic backdrop of what used to be called Ceylon, was too blasé to notice where she was in the world, the other too frightened to venture out in the streets on such a noisy occasion.

"I do think you're brave, Miranda!" she had said, her eyes enormous at the thought. *"Anything* might happen to you!"

"You might have your toes trodden on by an elephant," the other girl had added sourly. "I couldn't afford to have that happen to me, not on my side of the camera." She had preened herself, running her fingers through her hair, and had given Miranda a discontented look at the same time. "I can't think why you waste yourself taking pictures," she had gone on to say. "Your looks would come across quite well if you'd only do something about yourself!"

Miranda had laughed. She much preferred to be

the one who took the pictures. Indeed, she found it an embarrassment to be posed this way or that, in clothes she hadn't chosen for herself and which were almost always, in her experience, difficult to wear. She liked it better to be totally identified with the lens of her camera, uncaring of what she looked like herself. As she was now, in fact, her face innocent of any make-up, her fine, green eyes hidden behind her camera, and her black hair streaming over her shoulders and giving her an added anonymity in the moonlit darkness.

There was an open drain in front of her and she stood astride it to get a better shot of the caparisoned elephant who was to carry the cask containing the Sacred Relic. Other elephants, all richly clad and looking very like the little wooden, painted elephants that were for sale in all the souvenir shops all over the island, moved into the street to take up their positions, accompanied by a whirl of scarlet and gold that resolved itself into a group of dancers.

The groups of votive lights and flowers and fruits were in danger of being crushed by the new influx of spectators and Miranda was hard put to it to keep her place by the wall. She had been told at the desk of the hotel where she was staying that there were four minor *peraheras*, or processions, coming from the four devales, the shrines that are dedicated to the ancient deities who have the island under their protection and who are regarded as the servants of the Buddha by those whose beliefs had not yet advanced to acceptance to the pure doctrine of their Great Teacher. There was the procession of Natha, the buddha-to-be, there having already been four in our particular time-scale of which Gautama is the last; the procession of Vishnu, one of the three great Hindu gods; the procession of Skanda, the god of war and victory; and of Pattini, the goddess of chastity. The fifth procession, the largest and most magnificent of them all, carried the Sacred Tooth around the streets of the city the only time it ever left the sheltering walls of the temple that was dedicated to its protection.

Miranda was caught up in the beauty of the scene and began to press forward as did everyone else. There must have been a thousand or more dancers, their silver headdresses and beaded vests shimmering in the torchlight as they swirled backwards and forwards, offering their dance as an act of worship. Then there were the Chieftains, the lay custodians of the Sacred Tooth, walking in splendour, their dress that of a previous age with no less than forty yards of muslin draped about their waists. Every now and then they paused to receive the homage of the dancers and drummers, their fan-bearers and those carrying the umbrella betokening their rank pausing also and making patterns of colour in the surrounding darkness.

The elephants—perhaps a hundred of them—bejewelled and caparisoned emerged into the flickering torchlight, their bells tinkling and the howdahs swaying with every step they took. The mahouts, naked to the waist, sat easily on top of these heaving mountains, carrying plumed fans that waved back and forth and keeping an eye on the baby elephants who were there to learn how to conduct themselves in the future.

The most revered of these elephants, the Mali-gawa Tusker, was the focus of the whole procession. No mahout guided this beast. He walked alone, stepping with all the grace of his breed on the yards of white cloth that were laid out in front of him so that his feet would not touch the dirt of the street. So carefully did he walk that the casket containing the Sacred Tooth scarcely swayed at all under the silken umbrella that was covered again by a magnificent canopy held on high by men dressed in white carrying long poles.

Miranda pushed her way to the front of the crowd, belatedly recognizing that she had come a long way from her original position and was already hopeless-ly lost. For the first time she realised how foreign this crowd was to her. They were intent on something of which she had no knowledge, let along belief, and she spoke not a single word of their language. Supposing they became so stirred up by the combi-nation of noise and piety that they turned on her, a stranger? Supposing they resented her presence amongst them?

The whip crackers, clearing a path for the proces-sion to pass, chose that moment to come level with her and one of them, grinning at her startled face, cracked his whip within inches of her feet, making her jump. They did resent her! She turned to run away, little prickles of fear creeping up and down her spine. But there was no way of getting away. Everywhere were people with dark faces and flash-ing eyes illuminated by the torches they spun into the air and dexterously caught.

She took a step forward into the road and the

whip cracked dangerously about her ankles. Miranda would have snatched the length of leather away from him, but, perhaps fortunately, she panicked and could do no more than swing her camera in his direction. He caught it easily and would have pulled it away from her, accepting it as a gift, but an elephant came between them and he was forced to let go.

Miranda felt herself caught and held by the elephant's trunk, its breath warm against her face and the sparse hair pricking her. She gasped with fright as she was lifted off her feet and was deposited into the hands of the mahout seated on the enormous beast's neck.

"Let me go!" she screamed.

"It's a long way to fall," a deep, masculine voice warned her.

She looked down, terrified. It was indeed a long way down. She had never realised before how much higher an elephant was than a horse! She clutched at the restraining arm of the half-naked man behind her and heard him laugh.

"Take me back to my hotel!" she commanded him.

"Maybe," he said. "In time. Relax, my pretty one. You'll get a much better view of the proceedings from up here."

The truth of this only came to her gradually as her fright began to subside. She could see everything from her new perch, everything but the man who held her. Curious about him, she glanced down at the only part of him she could see, the strong muscled arm that held her, and was astonished to see that his hair shone gold as it brushed against her. He took her camera from her and slung it round his neck.

"How come you have blonde hair?" she asked him.

"How come you don't?" he retorted.

"I don't live here. You must or you wouldn't be driving this elephant."

"We have a reasonably mixed population," he murmured.

"Yes, I know," she replied, glad to show off her knowledge of the island. "There are the Singhalese, the Tamils, the Moslems from the Persian Gulf, even the Dutch." She hesitated. "Is that it? Are you Dutch?"

"No," he said.

She twisted her head round to look at him, feeling safer now she was growing used to being perched so high above the crowds. His hair looked silver in the moonlight and, when a blazing torch was flung up into the air beside them, she caught sight of the vivid blue of his eyes. His face was golden in the light of the torches. He scarcely looked human at all, with his finely chiselled face and jaw and the cruel twist to his sensuous mouth. Had his hair had been as black as hers, he would have looked even more like one of the Hindu gods she had seen peering down at Buddha seated under his tree in the temple murals.

His arm tightened like a band of steel about her and she was suddenly and intensely aware of him and the way he was holding her.

"Who are you?" she asked him again with increased urgency.

"My name is Adam Ferguson."

"An English name. What are you doing as a mahout in a Buddhist procession?"

"I came with the elephant," he explained. "She belongs to the tea factory that I manage a few miles out of Kandy. Her mahout went down with a fever last night and, as I'm the only other person she allows to ride her, I agreed to ride her in the procession. Our workers would have been disappointed if their elephant hadn't made her appearance in honour of the Tooth."

"Why couldn't someone else bring her?"

"She's half-wild. This is the only work she does, other than having her photograph taken by the tourists who come up here to see how we make tea. If she had someone she didn't trust up on her back, she'd run away from the noise. She's still very shy."

Miranda thought she hadn't been shy with her. The elephant had obeyed the order to lift her out of the crowd. She didn't know whether to be glad or sorry about that. It was a temptation to lean back against the golden chest and broad shoulders behind her and to allow the whirling crimson, silver and white of the dancers to take possession of her mind.

An oboe wailed in the distance and the pious cries of "Sadhu" were all about them. Somehow they had fallen behind, out of their place in the line, and were nearer to the elephant carrying the Sacred Casket than they had been.

"Mr. Ferguson, what made you pick me up?" she asked, in one of those strange silences that occasionally fell over the crowd.

"I wanted to."

She turned her head to look at him again. "Do you always do what you want?"

"With women I do."

Her eyes opened wide. "I nearly always get what I want too," she said.

"Then we're well matched. Call me Adam."

She swallowed, feeling less sure of herself. "I'm Miranda Wade."

"And what brings you to Kandy?" he enquired lazily.

"We're photographing a collection of clothes here. It's a very beautiful place and the idea is that the clothes will look better against a romantic background."

"With you as model I expect they do."

"But I'm not a model," she said flatly. "I take the photographs. You may have seen some of my work. I had a spread in—"

"Sorry, sweet, but I don't take the fashion papers."

"No," she answered, "I don't suppose you do. But it was quite a feather in my cap. I wouldn't have been asked to come out here if it hadn't been for that."

She could feel a tremor of laughter in his chest. "You're not taking many pictures now," he said.

"You have my camera." She didn't want to admit that she'd been too scared to do anything at first for fear of being pitchforked back into that seething, dark crowd below.

"I'm keeping it too. I don't like having to compete with any other interest when I take up with a woman."

"Have you taken up with me?"

"Well, I've taken you up. I may, or may not, take up with you when I've seen you properly."

The sound of the conches blowing just behind them covered her confusion. What if she didn't want to take up with him? The back of her neck prickled as she realised that, for the moment at least, she was very much at his mercy and she knew nothing whatever about him. He could be—

"Relax, you'll make the elephants nervous with that imagination of yours," he drawled in her ear.

"How d'you know what I'm thinking?" she demanded.

"I can tell by the set of your shoulders."

"You flatter yourself," she observed. "I sit up straight naturally and, if I'm nervous, it's only because I've never been up on an elephant before."

"Naturally."

What did he mean by that? She screwed round her head to look at him and was met by an imp of laughter in his eyes. She wished she could convince him she was quite accustomed to looking after herself but she suspected he was well aware that she had never been out alone in a foreign country before.

"I think the procession is coming to an end," she said with dignity. "Please take me to my hotel when it does so."

His arm tightened about her. "Where is the hotel? On the other side of the lake? You'll not get back there tonight. You'd best come home with me and the elephant."

She took a deep breath, steadying herself. Had

the noise and the colour and the verve of the dancers been too much for her? She had felt decidedly giddy for a moment. Of course it had passed, just as that fleeting moment of the evening's excitement was passing. Now she had to get back to her hotel and the relative sanity of the other girls. She should go to her bed and get a good night's sleep. But she wanted—she wanted to know this stranger a great deal better first.

"I don't think an elephant makes an adequate chaperon," she murmured. "I'll find my own way home to my hotel if you'll let me off somewhere near the bridge."

"My dear girl, you should have thought of that before! You shouldn't have come out alone like this in the first place, but since you did, you're stuck now with the consequences."

"What consequences?"

"Spending the night in my company," he said outrageously. "Think back to how you felt when I found you and ask yourself if you want me to turn you loose in the crowd again?"

Miranda preferred not to remember that moment of panic. "My friends will worry about me," she objected.

"You may telephone from my house. How is it they're not with you?"

"They wouldn't come," Miranda admitted. "I only came because I wanted to take some photos of the procession. I would have been all right—"

"Think again, sweetheart! You're better off with me!"

She caught the mocking look he gave her out of

the corner of her eye. "Am I?" she asked him. "Am I really?"

"Think of it as a splendid adventure," he advised, "and surely it must be reassuring to know I'm as British as you are?"

"I suppose so," she said dubiously.

He laughed. "Just what do you think I'm going to do to you?"

She preferred not to answer that question. He probably meant exactly what he said when he said she could spend the night at his house. He probably had a wife, or mother, who lived with him, so why should she worry?

"Well?" he prompted her. "Have you worked it all out to your own satisfaction?"

"Yes—if I really can't get back to my hotel, though I think I might do so if I waited for the crowds to clear. I wouldn't expect you to wait with me, of course, especially if you have to get home . . ."

"I do," he said firmly. "And I'm taking you with me! So be a good girl and talk about something else, if you must talk at all. Women always talk too much!"

"Too much for what?" she demanded.

His breath was warm against her cheek and she was again aware of the restraining arm that held her securely against him.

"I expect you'll find out before you're very much older!"

She turned her head to look at him. In the light of the flares he looked tall and impressive—almost god-like.

"Perhaps I already know," she said, ignoring the message of amused disbelief she read in his eyes.

They were coming back to the Temple of the Tooth now. The smell of burning copra and incense mixed with the sweeter smell of jasmine. The fervent crowd tossed their offerings together with garlands of flowers in the path of the carefully born casket they were all waiting to see, the golden casket carrying the relic of the Lord Buddha himself.

The drummers stirred themselves up into a frenzy of rhythm and sound as the elephant, the Maligwa Tusker, stood as if frozen in time while the casket was brought down from his back and taken back into the temple.

The silence that followed was disturbed only by the crowds as they tried to follow the Sacred Relic inside, scuffing off their shoes at the top of the temple steps.

"I'm sorry it's over," Miranda sighed. "I could have taken some better shots if I'd known exactly what was going to happen and had planned it all out in advance."

"You'd better come back tomorrow," Adam Ferguson advised her.

She stiffened. "With you?"

"Better than coming by yourself."

"Oh, but I couldn't," she said at once. "We have quite a programme to get through in the morning. We've chosen most of the settings, but there's still a lot of work to do before we even start on taking the photos. I shall have to be back at the hotel before breakfast."

"We'll see," he said mildly.

"We won't see anything! I have to be there I'm telling you!"

He moved his bare feet against the elephant's neck, grinning as he did so. "It'll be a long walk if I don't bring you. You'd have to start back as soon as we got there."

"But of course you'll bring me back!" The silence was so long that she added an uncertain "Won't you?" hopefully at the end.

"I may."

The elephant turned slowly, her eyes peering out of the holes provided in her elaborate caparison that covered her whole mountainous shape, even her trunk. In the torchlight, Miranda could see her eyelashes etched out against the dancing flame. She had never thought of elephants having eyelashes before.

"Of course you will!" she boosted her confidence. "Why wouldn't you?"

"I'll bring you back for the procession tomorrow night," he offered. "What's a day in the whole lifetime of days?"

"My days belong to my employers!"

"For the moment. It won't always be like that. Why don't you give tomorrow to me?"

She was tempted. She thought it might turn out to be the most beautiful day of her life, but they had little enough time in Sri Lanka as it was without any of them playing truant and upsetting the schedule.

"I can't," she said.

"I may take it," he warned her. "I want to get to know you better, Miranda Wade!"

Because he had been fleetingly attracted to her?

Because he always reached out and took what he wanted?

"I have to work," she repeated.

He turned off down a side-street, away from the noise and the fervency of the crowds. The elephant broke into a smart trot, glad to escape from the slow, deliberate pace of the procession.

"Let me off here!" Miranda ordered him firmly when she saw a landmark that she thought she knew, but he merely pressed the elephant on to greater speed and she was forced to cling to him to stay on at all.

They came to a sudden halt at the edge of the city. Adam Ferguson leapt lightly down onto the ground and went over to where he had parked his Range Rover earlier. He hooted the horn impatiently and, a few seconds later, a number of people came running towards him. Most of them looked like Tamils, the people who had been imported from South India to work the tea plantations in the time of the British. They were Hindus, not Buddhists, but that made not the slightest difference to their devotion to the Sacred Relic.

Miranda could feel their curiosity although they scarcely looked at her. They took charge of the elephant, palming their hands together and bowing their heads to Mr. Ferguson who not only returned their greetings but seemed to speak their language as easily as they did themselves.

"You'll feel more comfortable in the Range Rover," Adam invited her by opening the door on the passenger's side. "Some of these people are staying behind to look after the elephant, the rest are coming with us. I'm afraid it'll be a bit of a crush, but that'll all be part of the adventure for you, won't it?"

She eyed his charming smile suspiciously. "I'd rather be back with my own friends," she told him.

"So you will be—in time. Get in, Miranda, there's a good girl, or these people will think the less of you, arguing like any man, instead of doing as you're told as a woman should."

She opened her mouth to utter an indignant rejoinder, but his hand caught her round the elbow and she found herself seated on the front seat of the Range Rover whether she would or not.

"Move over onto the middle seat," he commanded her, and this time there was no charming smile, "and don't get in the way of the gears!"

The Tamil workers loaded themselves into the vehicle with great good humor. They packed the women and children into the back and the men shared the single available seat in the front next to Miranda or climbed up onto the roof, or anywhere else where they could find a place. In the end there must have been all of forty people clinging onto the Range Rover.

"Why won't you let me go back to the hotel?" Miranda demanded of Adam as he took his position in the driving seat.

"My dear girl, we've been through all that. We'd never get across the bridge. Don't you want to come with me?"

"No!"

He grinned. "Faint heart! I won't let any harm come to you!"

"We might not have the same definition of harm in mind," she said dryly.

It was too dark to see his expression, but she could feel the tension of his body next to hers and, to her dismay, she felt a wave of heat pass through her, leaving her breathless with her heart pounding against her ribs. Try as she would, she could not get the picture of his half-naked body, bronzed in the torchlight, out of her mind. She could still feel the iron strength of his arm around her, and she sighed involuntarily remembering his warm breath against the nape of her neck. She was surprised to hear Adam chuckle beside her.

"What's the joke?" she asked in a husky undertone.

"You are," he answered promptly. "A career lady you call yourself and you haven't even asked after your camera." His eyes glinted at her. "Had other things on your mind?"

"It's too dark to take photographs now," she defended herself. There was a long silence. "I'll take my camera now if you like," she went on.

But he only laughed out loud. "Tomorrow will be soon enough for that. Tonight I have other plans for you."

Chapter Two

Miranda had never seen a house anything like the one Adam Ferguson took her to. That he should call it a bungalow seemed quite ridiculous to her.

"A palace would be a better description!" she told him.

Adam only smiled. "I thought you'd like it," was all he said.

He watched her explore the sitting room, amused at her pretended indifference to her surroundings. The teak panelling impressed her despite herself, and the intricately carved Indian-type furniture that had a special scent of its own gave an air of wealth to the room.

In one corner of the room there was a collection of carved elephants, some of them made from ivory, some in wood and heavily jewelled. She stepped forward into the circle of light beside them to examine them more closely, amused to notice that yet others of them were no more than painted toys, somewhat the worse for wear, that could be bought in any of the souvenir shops across the island for a few pence. She wondered if Adam had had them as a child.

She turned her head to ask him about them and found him staring at her, his light eyes hard and unreadable. He was still standing in the shadows, but at the sound of her voice, he stepped forward beside her and for the first time she saw him in the full light.

The planes of his face betrayed a strong, unyielding character only contradicted by his full, sensual mouth. It was this feature that made her think uneasily that she was probably not the first woman who had been invited to spend the night at his bungalow.

He picked up one of the smaller, jewel-encrusted animals and stood it on the palm of her hand. "A keepsake from Nellie the Elephant to remind you of your ride on her back," he said. "No, don't put it back; put it away in your bag."

"But it's far too valuable! Please, I don't want such a present from you—I barely know you."

"You'll have plenty of time to get to know me," he suggested. "But in the meanwhile, which elephant would you accept?"

She grasped a tiny green painted elephant that missed the tip of its trunk. "I'd like this one please."

"One of my favourites," he said wryly.

Embarrassed, she sought to return the elephant to its place. "Oh, then, I'll take one of its brothers."

"A painted toy?"

"Yes, please."

"Not very demanding, are you?"

He came a step closer. She noticed he had thrown a shirt on over his naked torso.

"I don't really want to take anything from you at all," she admitted. "It was kind of you to bring me home with you—"

"Kind?"

"Wasn't it?" she asked him.

His eyes flickered over her with appreciation. "There's a shortage of your kind of company in Sri Lanka today," he said with a tight smile. "Why shouldn't I take advantage of a gift when it's offered to me?"

Miranda clenched her fists. "I think you've mistaken the package! I'm a liberated woman who earns her own living and makes her own way in the world. I make my own decisions."

His expression didn't change at all and she began to fiddle with the elephants to give her nervous fingers something to do. Her hair fell forward screening her face from him. When he put out a hand to lift the silken curtain, she drew back as if he had burned her.

"Now what's the matter?" he asked.

"You know very well!" she said in muffled tones. "I shouldn't be here—I should have insisted on going back to my hotel! I have to work in the morning, even if you don't!"

"Taking a few photos?"

"If you want to put it that way." Anger put steel into her backbone.

"Are you any good?" he asked brusquely.

"Yes, I am. I still have a lot to learn, but I wouldn't have got this assignment unless I was already well on my way."

His eyes glinted at her through the fringe of his eyelashes. "And what do you do for fun?"

"Fun comes later," she answered. "Much later."

"I wouldn't be too sure of that," he advised her.

She straightened her shoulders, looking him straight in the eyes. "I'm quite sure," she said firmly.

His hands gripped her shoulders, moving her inexorably towards him. "Perhaps now you will change your mind," he murmured against her cheek. His voice was low and aroused an answering quiver that she was unable to suppress. She felt her cheeks burn and hoped that he had not noticed her response. He pulled her face against his chest and she felt the roughness of the gold hairs against her skin. Now was the time, she knew, to protest. But somehow she could find no words at all with which to break the pulsating silence.

His hand cupped her chin, tilting her face up to his. The contact of his mouth against hers made her gasp, opening her mouth to his. She had been kissed before, but never like this. She felt as though she were drowning in sensations. She placed her hands flat against his chest, with the intention of pushing him away, but the feel of his skin and the smooth, hard muscles underneath excited her almost as much as his kiss had done. With no volition on her part, her arms crept up round his neck and she was holding him as fiercely as he was her.

"Now tell me you want to go back to your hotel!" he exclaimed in triumph.

Her eyes opened wide as she considered his words. Was it possible that he was right? She couldn't allow him to be right!

"You don't understand—" she began, backing away from him.

He caught her by the wrist and pulled her back into the circle of his arms. "What did you expect when you came with me?" he asked.

"I don't know. I didn't have any choice in the matter, did I? I asked you to take me back to the hotel, but you wouldn't! You made me come with you!"

"So I did," he acknowledged. "But I didn't think you really minded, Miranda Wade. You wanted to know me better just as I did you."

Was that true? That she had *wanted* to go with him?

"Well?" he prompted her.

"It was the procession. The noise—the colour and—and everything. It must have gone to my head," she excused herself. "But I'm quite sober now and I want to go back to the hotel this minute!" She sounded uncertain and lacking in determination even to her own ears. She made a last effort. "It isn't a lot to ask—" she began.

He cut her off. "Ring up your friends by all means, but here is where you're going to spend the night, Miranda Wade. Make up your mind to it!"

He strode out of the room into the hall, pointing out the antiquated telephone to her as he went.

She found a light beside the telephone and switched it on with a shaking hand. The telephone book was dog-eared and had several pages missing but, at length, she discovered the number she wanted and dialled it carefully. Within seconds she was connected with the reception desk of the hotel.

"Madam wishes to speak to Mr. O'Grady?"

"Yes please," Miranda confirmed.

There was a long pause, then, "Madam, are you still there? Mr. O'Grady has retired to bed. Shall I fetch one of the others in his party?"

"No," Miranda sighed. "I'm at the bungalow of Mr. Adam Ferguson. Could you arrange for someone to come and fetch me please?"

The receptionist made an impatient noise in the back of his throat. "You don't know what you're asking, madam," he said at last. "On any other night I would send a taxi, but tonight I cannot. This is the season of the great Kandy *Perahara* and the roads will be blocked all night. Mr. Ferguson will understand that you must remain a guest in his house for the night. I shall tell Mr. O'Grady where you are in the morning. Goodnight, madam."

The phone went dead with a sharp click.

"Is your Mr. O'Grady donning his armour to come riding to your rescue?" Adam enquired solicitously as she returned to the sitting room.

"No, he is not!" she returned shortly.

Adam's complacent features made her want to strike him. She could feel her fingers curling involuntarily into a fist. "Face it, Miranda, you're not going to get back to the hotel tonight!"

"I shall," she informed him through gritted teeth. "I shall, if I have to walk every step of the way!"

He put an arm around her waist. "I think not, my dear. You're staying here with me, whether you like it or not, and I rather think you do like it. Did you dine before you came out to see the *perahara?*"

"I'm not hungry."

"Some peoples' emotions always go straight to their stomachs," he agreed with ready sympathy. "I think I'll order dinner all the same. It may sweeten your temper."

"I shouldn't bank on it!"

His light eyes mocked her openly mutinous expression. "I'm not. What are you afraid of, Miranda Wade? Haven't you ever been alone with a man before?"

She licked her lips, wondering how to answer him. "Not all night," she said at last.

His eyebrows rose.

"I'm not staying!" she repeated, breathing deeply to steady herself. She brushed past him, seeking the front door and the safety of the night, but his arm held her back, forcing her once more into the circle of his arms.

"Not so fast, Miranda. We'll dine first and then I have someone I want you to meet."

"Your wife?"

"No, *not* my wife. A Mrs. Forster. Does that make you feel better about staying here?"

She eyed him suspiciously. "Won't Mrs. Forster eat with us?" she asked him.

"No, she keeps to her own room."

Her heart began to beat frantically against her ribs. He would be able to hear it soon, she thought in panic as a sweet ache of desire stirred within her, swelling and growling more urgent as the silence lengthened.

She could feel his hard arm against her back as he led her to a chair and settled her into it. He ran his fingers through her hair before straightening. "Black as night," he commented. "You're very beautiful, Miranda. Didn't you know?"

"I've never thought about it," she answered awkwardly, lowering her grey eyes.

"And no one has told you? Have you never been in love?"

The grey eyes returned to his face. "I haven't chosen yet to fall in love, no. One day, when I've done all the other things I want to do—"

"I could change your mind, Miranda. Would you like me to?"

"You don't know anything about me," she said primly.

"Enough."

She shook her head with determination. "No, you don't. This is the first big chance I've had to prove myself. Why should I throw it all away now? I want to do a book eventually. I'd like to do a book on Sri Lanka. But one has to eat while one learns and I sort of fell into fashion photography. I have the knack of making the clothes look good even if they're not. It's largely a question of making a pleasing picture with plenty of movement in it. It depends on the framing too. Some people can balance a picture by instinct and some never really get the hang of it."

Adam Ferguson looked thoughtful. "A book on Sri Lanka? What made you think of that?"

"It's the most beautiful place I've ever been to," she answered simply. "I long to make a lasting record of everything I've seen here."

"So why don't you do it?"

"I'm not ready yet."

"Who says so?"

"I do."

He sat on the arm of her chair. "Aren't you ready the moment you see the possibilities of doing such a thing?"

She shook her head. "I have to finish all my contracts first. I'm learning all the time. By the time I can clear the space to do it, it will be a better book, I'm sure of it."

He ran his finger down the side of her face and moved down to ease her collar from her neck. The movement brought a prickle of response to the surface of her skin. "Shall I talk to Mr. O'Grady in the morning and obtain your release?"

"No!" The word exploded out of her. "He'll tell you what I'm telling you now, that I have to work tomorrow—and the next day, and the day after that! And after that I'm due back in England to work some more!"

"I think I could persuade him to leave you behind here with me."

"Certainly not!"

He undid the top button of her shirt, his fingers warm against her skin. "Why not?" he murmured. "Don't you want to stay?"

Miranda swallowed. The ache of desire threatened to overwhelm her common sense. Pulling away from him, she buttoned her shirt with trembling fingers.

"I don't know anything about you!" she claimed.

He smiled with more than a touch of mockery.

"You know one thing about me, just as I know one thing about you."

She threw him a mute look of enquiry, her mouth dry. What could he possibly know about her?

"I want you," he answered her unspoken query. "And you want me too. I knew that as soon as Nelly rescued you from that crowd. You did feel it, didn't you, Miranda?"

She tried to avoid answering him, but she could not avoid the touch of his fingers on the side of her neck, nor the soft, feathering of them against the lobe of her ear. Desire that was almost a pain unfurled itself in the pit of her stomach. She wanted to hide her face against his neck, to turn into his arms as if she belonged there, and to let him do as he would with her.

"Miranda?" he said against her lips.

If she were to admit any such thing she would be lost. She closed her mouth tightly against his, pulling away from him.

"Please let me go!" she begged him.

He didn't hear her, or, if he did, he paid her no heed. His mouth was warm and unexpectedly gentle against hers, parting her lips with an ease that brought home to her her vulnerability as nothing else could have done. She wanted his kiss. She wanted his breath mingling with hers, and the feel of his tongue against hers.

"Oh, Adam!" she whispered.

He let her go reluctantly, his eyes amused as he watched while she struggled to return to some kind of normality.

"I think we'd better eat," he said. He stood up,

going over to the fireplace and ringing the bell. "Rice and curry do for you?"

"Thank you, that'll do very nicely."

A woman, dressed in a sari, came padding into the room, her bare feet making no sound against the hard-wood floor. Her soft, black eyes slid over Miranda and away again.

"Rice and curry for two," Adam ordered briefly. "And bring some fruit."

The woman bowed her head. "Will Mrs. Forster eat in her room?"

Adam's eyes narrowed. "You'd better ask her."

"I wondered if she would be joining you and your guest?"

"No."

The woman said nothing further, but the glance threw in Miranda's direction made Miranda wonder who Mrs. Forster was and what her relationship was to Adam.

"If Mrs. Forster prefers to eat with us—" Miranda began to say uncomfortably.

"I said no," Adam cut her off angrily. "This is still my house!" He turned back to the Singhalese woman. "Miss Wade is staying for the night. The procession prevented her from getting back to her hotel."

"I see. Shall I prepare a room for her?"

Adam's nod was brief. "And find her something to wear for the night, will you?"

"Yes, Mr. Ferguson."

Adam waited until she had gone, his mouth drawn into a tight line. "Does that convince you that you are adequately chaperoned for the night?"

Miranda shrugged. "Who is Mrs. Forster?"

"That woman's employer," he bit out viciously.

Miranda was astonished. "But, if the house belongs to you—?"

Some of the tension left Adam's body and he turned his whole attention back to her. "She has a certain right to be here," he told her wearily. "But don't let her presence worry you. She's my worry."

"I see," said Miranda, not seeing at all. She would have liked to have asked a great many more questions about the unknown Mrs. Forster, but good manners forbade it. She lapsed into silence, allowing Adam to find a new topic of conversation.

Adam, it seemed, had no wish to discuss Mrs. Forster with her. He went over to an ornate cabinet in one corner of the room and took out a bottle of Arrack, a drink made from the toddy that comes from the coconut flower.

"Have you taken to our local beverage?" he asked her.

"Only when it's heavily disguised with passion-fruit juice," she answered him.

He took her request seriously, dampening the edge of the glass and frosting it with sugar before half-filling it with the bright orange juice mixed with Arrack as she had requested. He filled his own glass with the same mixture and held it up to her in a silent toast.

Miranda took a sip, found it much stronger than she had expected, and very nearly choked over it. He came across the room and stood over her, smiling faintly. Nervously, Miranda took another, more cautious sip. He looked bigger than ever standing there between her and the light.

"Mr. Ferguson, I haven't thanked you—" she began, licking her lips.

"But then you don't feel particularly grateful, do you?"

"No," she agreed. "At least, I am in a way. I should have been happier to have gone back to the hotel—"

"Liar!"

"Mr. Ferguson!"

"Call me Adam," he invited her. He put a hand on the chair beside her and bent down until his head was on the same level as hers. "You called me Adam very nicely a few moments ago."

She willed herself not to blush. "How long will it be until dinner-time?" she enquired.

He straightened up, a muscle quirking with amusement in his cheek. "Only a few minutes," he assured her. "Sita will show you where to go. Ah, here she comes."

Sita escorted her down a corridor that ran at a right-angle to the hall and the long flight of grouped steps that led down to the front door.

"Can you find your own way back?" she asked, as she put out a clean towel in the bathroom.

"I think so," Miranda assured her.

It was strange how Adam's presence reached out to her throughout the whole house. The memory of how he had held her close against his bare chest, together with the lumbering movement of Nellie the elephant, came sharply back to her. She couldn't remember that she had ever felt so physically in tune with anyone else before. His touch had been like a shock of electricity passing through her. She could feel the tingle of it now as surely as she could feel the imprint of his mouth on hers, no matter how hard she scrubbed at it with the soap and water that had been put at her disposal.

When she returned to the sitting room, Sita was setting the table. Cut flowers decorated the snowy white tablecloth and the silver was old and heavy. Miranda made a movement to help her, but the Singhalese woman held up an imperative hand, commanding her to stay away.

To Miranda's surprise, Adam held her chair for her as she sat down at the table. She wasn't used to such attentions and she clutched at the napkin he spread across her knee, scared that it would fall to the floor. The smell of the food made her realise how very hungry she was. She inspected with approval the enormous bowl of rice, the slightly smaller one of curried meat, the home-made poppadums, and the rich mango chutney that came on the side. She piled her plate up high and then passed the serving spoons to Adam. The food at the hotel had been mostly English and she had found it rather dull, a relic of the years of the British Raj.

"I'm glad to see your adventures haven't ruined your appetite," Adam observed, helping himself in his turn.

"I like curry!" Miranda declared. "Besides, I've decided your bark is much worse than your bite. You haven't any intention of–of–" She sought a nice, neutral word.

"Violating your person?" he suggested dryly.

"Yes." She took a mouthful of curry, found it good and gave a sigh of content. "After all, you're English like myself, and there is Mrs. Forster!"

"You can't rely on my English blood," he advised her. "I've only visited there once in my life. I've always lived here, amongst other influences and other ideas. You may be in more danger than you think."

She shivered despite herself, her mouth gone dry. "I think I trust you all the same," she insisted.

He leaned back, the glint in his eyes very pronounced. "Are you appealing to my better nature? It's a waste of time, my dear. I learned to accept whatever gifts fate hands out to me long ago. The sooner you do the same, the happier you'll be here."

"I don't believe in fate," she said primly.

"That may be all very well in England, but in Sri Lanka we all have our astrological charts written out for us at birth. Our whole lives are organised by the stars; when and whom we marry, which day is propitious. When we are in danger, when we should go out, and when we should stay home. We have remarkably little say in what happens to us."

"I believe we are what we make ourselves," she retorted. "And so should you!"

"Why should I? The stars brought you to me. Ask Sita if you don't believe me!"

She wasn't sure if he were teasing her. "They may take me away again," she pointed out.

"You can choose to take an unpropitious path. One has free choice in that. But now that you are here, Miranda Wade, I won't easily let you go."

"You have to—first thing tomorrow morning! I have to get back to work!"

He looked at her in silence for a long moment. Then he moved his head and his light eyes sprang to life. She could see he had been laughing at her all the time.

"Maybe," he said.

Chapter Three

Miranda put her spoon and fork neatly together on her plate. She felt braver now that she had some solid food inside her.

"I know my future," she said. "I'm going to be a great photographer, successful with everything I touch!"

"Maybe," Adam said again.

"There's no maybe about it! I shall insist on it!"

His eyes played over her face and figure, undermining her confidence. *He has no right to look at me like that*, she thought with indignation. She had given him no cause to think that she would welcome his interest. Perhaps he looked at every woman in the same way.

"If you know when you were born, Sita will tell your fortune for you," he suggested. "It might be interesting to know what's in store for you. If you want to know more you'll have to go to the temple, but Sita has an uncanny knack of finding out the bare essentials."

"I don't believe a word of it!" Miranda denied. "Nor do you!"

"Perhaps," he conceded. "I neither believe nor disbelieve. I know better than to dismiss it out of hand, however. You can't live for long in the East and do that."

Sita was charmed to be asked to make out a simple astrological chart for Miranda. For a while she looked as if she almost approved of the previously unwanted guest. She sat down at the table and began laboriously to make out a pattern of symbols and writings according to the information she extracted from Miranda.

"You were born in May? At the time of the full moon. That is a very fortunate time to be born. It's when the Lord Buddha himself was born, the time when he was enlightened, and the time when he died. More babies are born at the time of the full moon than at any other time. It's like the tides of the sea, the moon pulls them out of their mothers. It has a great influence on the lives of us all."

She spoke with such certainty that Miranda became quite interested in the chart she was making for her after all.

"I was born a few minutes after midnight," Miranda told her.

Sita nodded her approval. "It will be hard for me to make this chart because you were born in England. The stars are in different places when viewed from there."

"Does it matter?" Miranda asked her.

Sita gave her an impatient look. "Of course it matters!" she snapped.

She was a long time gone before she came back with a much battered reference book from her own room. Armed with this, she was able to finish the chart more or less to her satisfaction.

"I can only tell you the main events," she murmured, "the monks could tell you more." She made some more hurried signs on the piece of paper in front of her. "May is a good month to be born and you will enjoy your life if you follow the right path."

"Will I be a famous photographer?" Miranda demanded.

Sita sniffed. "It's unimportant. Perhaps you will, perhaps you won't. It will depend on another as much as it does on yourself. You will not walk by yourself, unless you want to be sour and old before your time. You will be subject to another and in this lies your happiness. But you have the choice."

Adam chuckled. "Like Eve, you will be subject to Adam," he put in.

Miranda was outraged. "I beg your pardon!"

"Like the animals," he explained kindly. "Don't you remember how they passed before Adam and he gave them their names and they became subject to him?"

"You didn't name me!" Miranda said quickly.

"Not yet."

She wondered what he meant by that and came to the conclusion she preferred not to dwell on it. "I don't think that's very funny," she said.

Both he and Sita smiled imperturbably at her

indignant face. "It's written in the stars," Adam murmured.

"Nonsense!"

Sita pushed the chart across the table to where Miranda could see it for herself. "See! It is true what I have said! Look at where the planets are placed!"

"I don't want to!" Miranda protested.

Sita looked thoroughly bewildered. Adam motioned to her to leave the room and the woman went, slowly, frowning back at Miranda's flushed face.

"I didn't mean to upset her," Miranda defended herself, "but it's all a lot of nonsense—"

"And you don't want to believe it?"

"No!"

Adam looked amused. "It would seem you are far more upset than Sita," he remarked. "I wonder why?"

But they both knew why. She could read the answer in his light-grey eyes, and knew it in the restlessness of her own response to his lightest touch. She was upset because she was afraid that Sita had told her no more than the truth, that in some way totally outside her control Adam was for her as the North Pole is to a compass, pulling her where she would not go.

"I should never have come here!" she exploded angrily. "I knew it was a mistake!"

Adam rose to his feet. "Cheer up, Miranda, you will be back at work tomorrow—"

"Will I?" She sighed. "I hope so. This job is more important to me than anything I've ever done before. I don't want it spoilt! Please don't spoil it for me!"

He caught her hand in his and pulled her to her feet beside him. "I think it's time you went to bed—"

"Alone!"

He lifted an eyebrow, giving her a mocking look that was very disturbing to her. "My dear girl, shouldn't you wait until you're asked?"

She might have known he would put her in the wrong. The warm colour rose in her face and she pulled her hand free of his, putting it behind her back in a defensive gesture as if she were afraid he would take it back again.

"You and Sita would say I didn't have any choice—" she began on a note of desperation.

"Have you?"

"Of course I have! I shall go back to the hotel tomorrow and I shall never see you again!"

He shook his head at her. "I want you, Miranda Wade."

"You have Mrs. Forster!"

"But it's you I want."

If she had known which room had been prepared for her, she would have turned and run, but the thought of getting lost in this immense house prevented her. Also, she might burst in on Mrs. Forster. Even though she was curious as to who exactly Mrs. Forster was, she did not want to meet her under such circumstances.

"I'm tired," she said aloud. "I think I will go to bed."

"As you wish. Do you want a hot drink to go to bed with?"

"No thank you."

His eyes narrowed. "What do you want?"

She wanted for him to hold her and kiss her again. She wanted the evening never to end, to be just the two of them for ever and ever. She caught herself with a rasping breath that hurt her throat.

"I'm tired. I want to go to bed," she said in even tones. "Alone."

"Oh, Miranda!" he mocked her. "How long are you trying to convince yourself of that?"

"For as long as necessary!"

His face was so close to hers she could feel his warm breath against the curve of her cheek.

"Don't you want to sleep in my arms and be loved by me?" he murmured.

"It wouldn't be love! I barely know you!"

He trailed his fingers along the line of her jaw. "Little prude," he reproved her. "What are you afraid of?"

"I'm not afraid!" she declared. "I'm certainly not afraid of you!"

"No? Of yourself then?"

She would have denied that too, but it was so very close to the truth. "I'm not that sort of person. I have my career and, later on, when I want to get married—" she sputtered.

His fingers closed over her chin. "You don't know yourself at all, my girl," he informed her in the same intimate tone he had used all along. "Your career has served its purpose in bringing you here to me.

Doing your book on Sri Lanka will make a nice hobby for you."

She summoned up her will to move away from him, but her body refused to obey her mind's commands. His arm slipped round her and pulled her close against the wall of his chest.

"Are you going to object to my kissing you goodnight?"

Drugged by his closeness, a river of excitement spread through her veins. She opened her mouth to voice some objection, but no words came out. Instead his mouth came down on hers in a hard, determined kiss that left her gasping for breath. She found her body curving itself against his as though this was what it had been created for. He held her closer still as her brief resistance flared and died, changing into a delicious surrender that made her tremble against him. His hands explored her back and the soft curves of her breasts and she dug her fingers into his hair at the nape of his neck. It was a long, long time before he let her go. "You kiss very well," he commended her. "A little practice and no man will ever ask for more."

She caught her lower lip between her teeth. "That'll be just as well because I wouldn't give him any more!" she said.

He gave her a little shake. "You may not be given the choice," he warned her.

She blinked, trying to ignore the craven desire to creep back into his arms. "I've never kissed anyone like that before—" she began.

"There has to be a first time," he answered her, with such gentleness that she felt like crying.

"You don't understand! I can't afford this kind of thing!"

"Miranda, my love, you may not have any choice. You're beautiful and, whilst you may be without any experience in these matters, the same can hardly be said of me."

Mrs. Forster! Obviously she shared not only his house but also his bed.

She tore herself away from his restricting hands. "I live my own life, Mr. Ferguson, and these sordid little games aren't part of it!"

"Sordid, Miranda? You can do better than that!"

"No, I can't. I'm trying to tell you that I don't go in for love affairs and things like that—"

"Particularly things like that?" he mocked her, trying not to laugh.

"Yes."

"I'm immune to men at the moment," she added. "I'm into photography instead."

He laughed out loud. The sound of it whirled about her ears. She wiped the damp palms of her hands against the sleeves of her shirt, wondering how she could convince him.

"If you're immune," he asked her dryly, "why are you so nervous of me, Miranda Wade? Face facts, my dear. You're far too beautiful for men to leave you alone for long. You'd do far better to find one who'll protect you from the rest."

"I can look after myself!"

"If you want to go to bed by yourself, don't tempt me to prove you wrong, Miranda. You do want to go to bed by yourself, don't you?"

"Yes!"

His smile was wicked and the glint in his eyes made her heart pound with a painful excitement that brought a trembling to her limbs and turned her bones to moulton wax.

"We'll see how you feel about things in the morning," he said comfortably. "I don't want you throwing it in my face that I took advantage of you in a weak moment, reluctant as I am not to persuade you back into my arms. Come on, and I'll show you to your room!"

Miranda never knew how she pulled herself together sufficiently to follow him out of the living room and down one of the endless corridors to the bedroom which had been prepared for her. She had no idea which way they went, she was far too engrossed in the magnitude of her own thoughts. *Could* he have persuaded her to fly in the face of her upbringing and all her better instincts? She was very much afraid that he might be right about that, as he had been right about so much else about her. It was not a thought to dwell on.

The bedroom which had been prepared for her smelt of wood and polish. The frame of the bed was made from solid wood, carved and beautiful, and the flooring had been polished until it looked like glass. The curtains and bedding were made from local products, the curtains of batik cottons, the bedspread dyed in the brilliant colours beloved by those who live in the tropics.

"Will it do?" Adam asked her.

She turned in protest at the question. "It's perfect. You have a lovely house, Mr. Ferguson, as you very well know."

His lips twitched. "Perhaps that's why I feel the need of a lovely woman to go with it," he remarked.

"What about Mrs. Forster?"

He walked over to the window and threw open the shutters, and the sounds of the night came flooding into the room.

"Mrs. Forster doesn't belong to me," he answered wryly, as he moved towards the door.

"And that makes a difference?"

He turned and looked at her and she was very aware of the clean-cut lines of his face and the extraordinary length of his lashes against his cheeks. "Goodnight, Miranda."

"Goodnight, Mr. Ferguson."

"Adam," he corrected softly, as he closed the door behind him.

Miranda thought she wouldn't sleep a wink in that enormous, strange bed, but she fell asleep almost at once. She was still asleep when Sita brought her a glass of freshly squeezed orange-juice the next morning and announced that breakfast would be served on the verandah in half-an-hour's time.

"What time is it?" Miranda asked her, yawning.

"It will be seven very soon. Mr. Ferguson said you had to be away early."

"Yes, I do. Will I see Mrs. Forster before I go?"

Sita's face gave nothing away. "Mrs. Forster has no interest in Mr. Ferguson's guests. She is here on business about the plantation."

Miranda sat up on one elbow. "Doesn't Mr. Ferguson manage it? Is Mrs. Forster the owner?"

"Her husband—"

Miranda wondered why it hadn't occurred to her that Mrs. Forster might have a husband. "Is he here too?"

Sita shook her head. "He never comes here now," she said with tight disapproval. "It has made Mrs. Forster very unhappy that he won't have anything to do with the tea that is grown here. It has always been her whole life."

"Was she brought up here in Sri Lanka?" Miranda asked.

"She and Mr. Ferguson."

"Together?"

"They have always known each other," Sita answered, astonished that anyone should not know this basic fact about her employers. "Will you be able to find your way to the verandah?"

Miranda nodded, a great deal more confident now that it was day again and the romance of the procession, the full moon, and the extraordinary effect Adam Ferguson had had on her, safely belonged to the night before.

"I'll find it," she said.

Miranda lost no time in dressing herself, folding the nightdress she had been loaned for the night and putting it neatly on the bed. She was curious to see what the bungalow looked from the outside. The view from her bedroom window was an enticing one. Sweeping green lawns and exotic flowers gave way to distant tea bushes broken only by the ornate tower of a small Hindu temple.

She found the verandah quite easily in the end and was disconcerted to see that Adam was there before her. It was the first time she had seen him in daylight. He was a large-framed man, dressed in a pair of close-fitting green trousers, topped by a lighter green shirt which was open almost to the waist. Standing there in the sunlight he looked a magnificently powerful male animal. She realised she was staring at the gold matt of hair on his chest in which some kind of medallion was almost lost.

He put a hand on it, holding it out to her. "I've worn it all my life," he told her. "My *ayah* gave it to me when I was a baby."

"What is it?" she asked, refusing to take a closer look.

He shrugged his shoulders, taking it off and placing it around her neck. "It brings the blessings of the Hindu gods with it. We all partake as far as we can of each other's religious practices in Sri Lanka, the Buddhists, the Hindus, and the Christians. One day I'll take you up to Adam's Peak—"

"You have a peak of your own of course!" she interrupted him.

"Of course," he agreed. "With a shrine at the top."

"I'd like to see it for myself—and take some photographs," she mused to herself.

"If you kiss me good morning, I'll take you," he offered.

"No, thank you."

His eyes gleamed with amusement. Seen in the sunshine they were a light grey, broken with patches of a hazel hue that fascinated her because they were never the same for two minutes put together.

"Coward!" he accused her.

"Not at all," she denied with dignity, seating

herself on one of the whicker chairs that looked out across the gardens. "Merely a busy, working girl with a job to do."

"Ah, yes," he said, "I thought we would come back to that!"

"I can hardly do anything else seeing it's the whole reason for my being in Sri Lanka. I *like* my work!"

"So you keep telling me. I doubt if you will find it enough for you for much longer though." He leaned forward with a suddenness that made his chair creak. "Will you?"

"Why shouldn't it be?"

"You were meant for other things—"

She retreated into the depths of her chair. "What things?" she asked in a muffled voice.

"You don't need a profession," he said flatly. "You need a man, one who will demand of you everything you have to give, who will make you wholly his—in every way!"

She averted her flushed face, making a pattern with her finger on her knee to give herself courage. To her consternation his hand closed over hers, his fingers threading themselves through hers.

"You shouldn't say such things!" she reproved him. She tensed her muscles until they ached with the effort. "I'm not open to that kind of proposition. Even if I were not here to work, I don't want to get involved in a temporary—"

"It was a statement of fact, not a proposition."

She was more confused than ever. It had sounded like a proposition to her. He had told her he wanted to make love to her, so what else could it have been?

"I don't need a man at all!" she claimed wildly.

His lips met hers in a kiss so brief that it had ended long before she had time to defend herself from its impact.

"You'd better eat your breakfast," he said, "if you want me to take you back to your hotel before I start work."

She saw that Sita was bringing a laden tray out onto the verandah and hurried to help her, glad of the excuse. There was a plate of slices of papaya and pineapple mixed, some hot croissants, butter and marmalade, and a pot of coffee that filled the air with its fragrant smell.

"Will you have a boiled egg, or eggs and bacon?" Sita asked her.

Miranda shook her head. "I love having fruit for breakfast. I'd never had papaya before I came here. It looks delicious and tastes wonderful!"

Sita smiled her approval. "Sprinkle on some lime-juice, that is the best way," she recommended.

Miranda did so, eating the orange-coloured melon-shaped fruit with gusto. There were many things she would regret leaving behind in Sri Lanka when it was time for her to leave, she thought, but it would be the exotic fruits that she missed most of all. She didn't even bother to look up when she heard the french-windows opening again, thinking it was Sita coming back with Adam's bacon and eggs, but it was someone else who came over to the table, flinging herself into a vacant chair. This was one of the loveliest women Miranda had ever seen, beautiful in a brittle, frail way that was appealing even before she saw the lines of unhappinness etched into the other woman's face.

"I'm Anne Forster," the woman said. "Who are you?"

Adam barely looked at the newcomer. "This is Miranda Wade. Nellie and I picked her up yesterday during the procession."

"And you brought her back here?"

"Her hotel is on the other side of the bridge."

Anne Forster closed her mouth into a tight line. "One excuse is as good as another. How long is she staying?"

Miranda looked at her and disliked her. "I'm leaving in a few minutes," she answered for herself. "I have a job of work to do."

Mrs. Forster's glance was cynical. "I'm sure you have, my dear, but Adam always gets his own way in the end—even with the busiest of busy little bees. I should know! I wouldn't be here now if it weren't for him!"

Chapter Four

"You don't live here all the time then, Mrs. Forster?" Miranda said uncomfortably.

"I do now. Adam wishes it."

"If you won't live with John—" Adam began to speak.

"Let's not go into that again," Mrs. Forster stopped him wearily. "You know why I can't do that."

"Do I?" Adam's eyes were hard, even while he was smiling. "Are you ready to go, Miranda?"

"Yes."

"Come on then, let's go."

He hurried her through the house, scarcely allowing her to pick up her handbag. She wondered what it was about Mrs. Forster that had such an effect on him. Was there something between them after all?

"Where is Mrs. Forster's husband?" she asked

him as he pushed her, none too gently, into the front seat of the Landrover.

"In England."

She turned wide eyes on him. "But she lives here?"

"Yes, she lives here. Satisfied?"

She wasn't, but neither did she have the courage to question him further. Anne Forster's obvious unhappiness only added to her haunting beauty. She was painfully thin, which probably made her eyes seem so large and tragic, but they were beautifully shaped as well, as were all her other features. Her colouring was unusual too, with that bright orange hair like spun silk and a milky white skin that was spoilt only by its unhealthy pallor. She should get out more, Miranda told herself wisely, get out and about in the sun and meet more people.

The country they were driving through was incredibly beautiful. The sides of the hills were almost all planted with tea bushes and, in some of them, women in colourful saris and with great baskets balanced on their backs, were picking the new leaves, methodically moving up and down between the bushes under the direction of their forman.

There was water in many of the valleys, small streams that fell over the rocks in waterfalls, looking cool and pretty beneath the hot sunshine. The early morning mists had already burned away and the sky was blue and cloudless. It was going to be a terrific day for photography.

"Are you in love with her?"

She wished the words unsaid as soon as she heard them coming out of her mouth. How could she ask him a thing like that? Hadn't he already made it quite clear to her that Mrs. Forster was none of her business?

"Would you mind if I were?"

She couldn't believe her ears. "Why should I?" she retorted, stung because she did mind though she couldn't think why she should. Adam Ferguson meant nothing to her!

"You tell me, Miranda Wade."

She sank back into silence. They turned a corner and a tea-factory, clinging against the side of the hill, came into view some way below them.

"Is that where you send your tea?" she asked him.

"No, we have our own factory. We're very high where we are and we grow a very expensive tea. The quality is less good the further down you go—though this is still of export quality. It's better than most of the mixes you can buy in England."

"But not as good as yours?"

"No. Most people can't afford to drink our tea. Retail in London it would work out at about twenty-five dollars a pound—about ten pounds a pound."

"I might have known," Miranda sighed. "I prefer ordinary tea."

"That's because you've never tried mine. Next time you come I'll make you a pot of tea that will change your mind. When are you coming again?"

She wriggled in her seat. "I'm not. I won't be here for much longer—"

"I'll pick you up tonight and show you the procession from the very beginning. Will you dine with me first?"

She shook her head. "You know I can't. Besides, I saw all I want to of the procession last night. I can't play truant every night I'm here."

"You can still dine with me."

"I'd rather not."

"She felt close to tears and she sniffed, hoping he wouldn't notice. He stopped the Landrover by the side of the road and turned and looked at her.

"I'll pick you up at six-thirty. There's no need to cry about it, Miranda."

"I'm *not* crying!"

He caught a tear on his forefinger and held it up to her. "No?"

"It's—it's the dust and everything!" she explained.

His fingers caught the point of her chin and he turned her face up to his. "Are you sure it isn't because you think you may never see me again if you don't dine with me tonight?"

"Quite sure!"

She was mesmerised by the firm curve of his mouth, watching it flirt with a smile of amusement.

"Your eyes change colour when you tell lies," he observed. "Why are you afraid of falling in love? I don't believe this career of yours is as important to you as that."

She sighed, afraid of what else he might see. "There's no future in my falling in love with you," she said. "And I don't intend to! I'm going back to England as heart-whole and fancy free as I was when I came here!"

He smiled then, his eyes lighting up with a peculiarly masculine triumph. "It's too late for that," he told her. "There's something between us, whether you want it or not. You won't escape me easily, Miranda Wade."

She pushed herself away from him, gripping the handle of the door with her hand until it hurt. "We'll see about that!" She forced a light smile to her lips as if she hadn't a single care in the world. "You're far too sure of yourself, Adam Ferguson!"

He shook his head. "I'm sure of you," he contradicted her. "Will you be ready at half-past-six?"

She ought to say no, she had every reason to no, but she did nothing of the sort. She hung her head, glad of the curtain of hair that fell forward, hiding her face from him.

"Why don't you take Mrs. Ferguson out to dinner?"

"Because I'm taking you." He pushed her hair back over her shoulders. "Don't be difficult, Miranda. I have to ride Nellie in the procession but, apart from that, I intend to spend the whole evening with you. Nothing else will do for either of us, will it?"

Her eyelashes fluttered as she sought for the right answer. She knew she would go with him, probably eager and ready, at least half an hour before the specified time, but she didn't want him to know that.

"I'll bring my camera," she said at last.

"You do that!" he mocked her. "You may even take a few pictures tonight."

She managed a rather wobbly smile. "I'll take some of you and Nellie—to remember you by!"

His fingers leaned against her cheek. "I don't think you'll forget me, Miranda. . . . His eyes caught hers for a long moment before he turned away to start the Landrover again to rattle on downwards towards Kandy. Miranda sat forward eagerly anticipating her first sight of that small jewel of a city, and she was not disappointed. There was the Temple of the Tooth reflected in the lake, the bridge that joined the two sides of the town together, and over it came a line of Buddhist monks, their saffron robes a bright yellowy-orange in the sunshine, their begging bowls in their hands, as they returned from their morning round to allow the people to gain merit by giving them food.

Miranda jumped nimbly down to the ground as Adam drew up outside her hotel. "Half-past-six?" she checked with him.

He nodded. "Bring a toothbrush and anything else you'll need for the night. The roads will be blocked again tonight."

Panic stirred somewhere in her middle. "Then I won't come!"

"Be here, at half-past-six, Miranda, or I'll come and find you!" he warned, as he put the Landrover back in gear.

She had no doubt that he meant what he said. She could imagine him combing the hotel for her and upsetting Liam O'Grady, and when Liam was upset, everything went wrong. Poor Mr. O'Grady was harrassed enough trying to keep the party together as one happy family, as he liked to put it. He expected his models to give him trouble, but for Miranda to do so would be regarded as an act of treachery of the worst kind. He liked Miranda. In fact, Miranda had occasionally suspected he more than liked her. But she felt nothing for him but liking and she tried to put these suspicions out of her mind.

She watched the Landrover depart with a cold feeling in her heart. She felt as though she didn't belong to herself any more, but what did she know about Adam to make her think that she should even consider giving up a perfectly good career for him? She felt confused. She didn't know what it was that Adam wanted of her, or what she wanted for herself. Oh, she knew that he wanted to make love to her, to share her bed for a night or two, but did that mean he wanted to have a more lasting relationship with her? What about Anne Forster? She couldn't get Anne out of her mind. She was appalled to realise that she was actually jealous of unhappy, lovely Anne, more jealous than she had ever been of anyone before.

The day passed in a whirl of activity. Whatever curiosity the girls might have displayed about where Miranda had spent the night was sternly nipped in the bud by Liam O'Grady.

"We're here to work!" he reminded them all a hundred times every hour. "Please get on with it!"

And work they had! Miranda had lost count of the number of poses she had set up, pleading, cajoling, bullying the two girls to look this way and that, to run and jump until she had obtained a certain rippling effect with one of the skirts; then to sit in acute discomfort on the sharp rocks above the lake whilst she waited for the sun to reach a particular spot in the sky. They were all exhausted when they returned to the hotel.

"Are you going to see the procession tonight?" Miranda asked the two models.

"Are you joking? I'm going to have a hot bath and lie about doing nothing after the day you've given us!"

Miranda wondered if she had driven them too hard. "We have so little time," she began to explain, but neither girl was in the mood to listen.

"Give me a male photographer every time," they agreed with one another. "They listen when you say you're tired and have had enough!"

"Sometimes!"

"It's all part of the job!" Miranda reminded them cheerfully. "You shouldn't do it if you don't like looking cool and beautiful under a burning sun."

"What do you know about it?" they jeered. "All you have to do is press the button!"

It was dark when they got back to the hotel. Miranda glanced at her watch and saw she had less than half-an-hour in which to get ready for Adam. She could hear the noise of the procession forming in the town and felt a little shiver of anticipation of the evening before her. What should she wear? What had Adam meant when he had said he couldn't let her go?

Indecision had an enervating effect on her. She, too, was tired from the long day in the sun, but that was no good reason why she couldn't make up her mind whether she should wear a pair of jeans or an evening dress! Cross with herself for this unwonted display of indecision, she took a cold shower, allowing the water to spray over her heated body until she was numb and uncaring of what she would say to Anne Forster if she should be there for dinner also.

When she came out of the shower, she pulled a towel about her and padded back into her room. She knew the instant she pushed the communicating door that the room was no longer empty, but it was too late to draw back.

"Who is it?" she demanded, pleased that she should sound so confident.

"It's after half-past-six," Adam's voice reminded her.

She stood stock still in the doorway, a wave of shock passing over her at the pleasure it gave her to see him. "Shouldn't you be waiting downstairs?" she asked in even tones.

"I told you I'd come looking for you."

He was bare-footed, dressed in a shirt and the local skirt-like garment tied tightly in a knot around the waist, which constantly had to be re-tied for comfort. His shirt was open and the gold hairs of his chest were plainly in view. He looked powerful and very handsome and it took an effort of will for Miranda to tear her eyes away from the sight of him. She lifted her towel higher over her breasts and licked her lips to give herself time to make some stinging retort.

But as usual he had already read her mind. "Is that what you're planning to wear?" he asked her.

She backed into the bathroom, her cheeks hot. "If

you'll pass me my clothes, I'll get dressed in here,"
she told him.

"Little prude," he commented. "Which of these
garments do you want?"

She hitched her towel more firmly about her and
marched into the bedroom and over to the bed
where she had put out the two choices of what
she would wear. She grabbed the nearest bundle of
black velvet trousers, a snowy-white, lace-edged
shirt, and a length of black shoe-string to tie round
her neck.

"I'll take these." She grabbed her underwear and
retired to the refuge of the bathroom.

When she emerged a couple of minutes later, he
was lying on her bed, his long legs crossed and at his
ease, balancing the little elephant he had given her
on his chest.

"I wish you'd go downstairs!" she said angrily.

His eyes narrowed and she could see them glinting
through his lashes. "Would you prefer I kissed you
good evening in public?"

"I'd prefer it if you didn't kiss me at all!"

He reached out a hand to her. "Come here,
Miranda," he commanded her.

"Certainly not!" Her voice trembled, but her face
gave nothing away as she turned her attention to the
dressing-table and began brushing her hair into a
more suitable style for the evening.

He moved with the speed of lightning, his hand
catching her wrist and, pulling her off balance, he lay
back, forcing her down on top of him.

"Better give in now, Miranda Wade," he warned

her. "I'm not a patient man and you've already kept me waiting all day."

"Waiting for what?"

She regretted the question as soon as she had uttered it. She could hardly fail to recognise the leaping of his senses in conjunction with hers. The warm hardness of his body beneath hers stirred a previously unknown desire within her to come closer still to him, to reach her arms around him, and to press her lips to his.

"'I want you, Miranda." His eyes were fully open now, the hazel patches in them concealing the cooler grey and burning into her.

"Well, you can't have me!" she said quickly.

"No?"

The single syllable set her heart racing. She fell victim to the temptation of rubbing the palm of her hand against his chest and he groaned as she did so, his arms tightening about her and easing her onto her back beside him until their positions were reversed and it was she who was supporting the greater part of his weight. One hand separated her shirt from her trousers and moved upwards to the slope of her breast, exploring where it would.

She had no defence against him. Her mouth opened to his as if she was starved for the taste and feel of him and she made no effort to stop him as he caressed her more intimately.

"Is it still no?" he asked her.

She took a deep breath, trying to regain control of her errant senses. To pull away from him now would be like tearing herself in two and she was ashamed of this new weakness that wanted only to please him and to give him whatever he chose to take from her.

Her silence made him look more closely and he saw the hint of tears back of her eyes. He let go, turning his back on her, his face grim.

"Why not, when you want me too?" he demanded.

"I don't know." Her voice was shadowed and she thought her heart was about to break in painful pieces. "I'm not ready—"

"How long does it take you for you to be ready for love?"

"But it isn't love!" she protested. "Love doesn't happen in a moment, like a thunderclap. If I thought you loved me—"

He turned and faced her. "You can't run away forever, Miranda. Your own feelings won't let you do that. You want me too. If I let you go now, there'll be other times—possibly even tonight. It's your destiny to be loved by me sooner or later!"

She threw her arm up over her face, blocking out the sight of him. "You talk of love, but you mean something else."

"What do you know about it?" he asked her. "Is it lust you feel for me?"

Was it? How could she tell? She stirred uneasily beneath his hand. "What else can it be?"

He kissed her hard on the lips. "Poor Miranda, don't you know? You'd better find an answer to the problem quickly before I resolve it for you. Think yourself lucky we have a procession waiting for us or you might not escape so lightly!"

When he let her go, she longed for the warmth of his body against hers. There was a need within her that ached for fulfilment. It would be good to ride in the procession with him again, she thought, anything not to be alone with him until she was her normal self again.

She brushed her hair until it cracked with electricity and then combed it flat, smoothing it back behind her shoulders. Her mouth looked bruised, she noticed in the glass, and hoped they wouldn't run into the others on their way out of the hotel. It was just the kind of thing that either of the two girls would notice and they would give her no peace until they had heard all the details of who had kissed her and when.

"I'm ready," she said at last.

His eyes flickered approvingly over her as he retied his sarong around his waist, folding the corners in against his stomach.

"You look good enough to eat!" he complimented her. "Beautiful and wholesome and very, very sweet."

She lowered her eyes. "I'd rather be sexy and mysterious." Like Mrs. Forster, she added to herself.

His mouth quirked. "You'll do as you are!"

She went out the door still not looking at him, leaving it to him to lock her room and bring down the key. If she had stayed, or if she had allowed herself to dwell on his appearance as he had dwelt on hers, she would have begged him to—to do what? Her face burned with embarrassment at the thought.

What would she have said to him? Please make love to me and never mind the procession? How would she have lived with herself after that?

Nellie the elephant was waiting for them in the queue of cars that was lining up outside the hotel. Miranda recognised the man who was with her as one of the Tamil workers from the evening before. She was rather touched when he greeted her with a low bow and a wide grin, palming her hands together in a joyous gesture that made her feel he was really glad to see her.

Half the hotel came pouring out to see the elephant. Flash lights popped as Adam bade the great beast hold out one of her front legs and leaped nimbly up onto her neck. He looked completely at home up there, uttering his commands in a few gutteral syllables that made Nellie toss her trunk from left to right and lift up her leg again.

Adam reached down his hands and Miranda put her own out to him and felt herself swung off the ground and up to get first a foothold on the elephant's leg and then to take her place in front of him. His arm came round her to balance her better against his thighs and the elephant began to walk forward, swaying slightly from side to side.

It was at that moment that Liam O'Grady came rushing out of the hotel.

"*Miranda!*"

She waved to him, annoyed that he should have seen her. She could well imagine the endless questions she would have to face in the morning. Liam was genial enough when nothing happened to cross him, but he felt his responsibilities towards the female members of his group very deeply and he would not approve of her taking part in the local life of Kandy when she should have been getting her beauty sleep, or at least developing the shots she had taken that day. He didn't approve of slip-shod work, even less did he approve of members of his party who didn't check their every action with him first before they went gallivanting round the countryside.

"What time will you be back?" he demanded, craning his neck to look up at her.

"I'll be there when you want to start work in the morning," she promised, crossing her fingers as she hoped she was speaking the truth. It would be just like him to want to start at six o'clock to catch the dawn!

"But what *time* will you be back?" he repeated the question, dismissing her answer as absurd.

Adam leaned down towards him, using the elephant to push Mr. O'Grady back into the line of the other onlookers.

"She may not be back at all," he drawled. "She'll be with me when you want her!"

"And who might you be?" Liam shouted after them.

Adam raised his hand high in a final salute. "Adam Ferguson of the Mahawell Tea Estate. Anyone will tell you where to find me."

They were all there now, the whole crew, including the two models, their mouths open with astonishment. Miranda made a movement towards them, but Adam merely held her more tightly against him.

"Adam, they'll think—" she began to plead with him.

"They'll only think the truth," he answered, "that you've thrown in your lot with me. You're mine, Miranda, and mine you're going to stay!"

And, with his arm about her and with his hard muscles supporting her as the elephant moved beneath them, who was she to argue with him? It was what she wanted too, wanted it more than anything in the world—to be subject to Adam!

Chapter Five

Anne Forster was wearing a cotton kaftan dress. She was standing on the verandah looking out across the moonlit garden.

"I never interfere with anything Adam does," she was saying. "He has always been his own master. The rest of us have never had a say in anything—"

"I can imagine!" Miranda agreed, laughing. "We're all the subjects of King Adam in his opinion."

"But you don't have to be!" Anne said quickly. "You can leave here any time you choose. You're making a big mistake to trust Adam further than you can see him."

Miranda had the uncomfortable memory of Adam calling out to Liam O'Grady that she would be with him. She had argued with him about that the whole way to the temple. She had a job of work to do and he had no business making it more difficult for her.

"I want you here with me," he had answered stubbornly.

"Then want will have to be your master!" she had snapped at him.

"Not all the time I'm yours," he had told her dryly.

What Miranda might have said then she would never know. Perhaps it was as well that the drums had started up close beside her, their deafening roar making any conversation quite impossible. She had been indignant—of course she had been indignant!—but it had seemed less important to her while the procession had been moving forward than it did now when it was all over.

If she had known Anne Forster better, she might have asked her to tell her more about Adam, but there was something about the fragile Anne that she didn't trust, even less like, though she had gone out of her way to be pleasant to Miranda all evening.

"I'm only here for the evening," she said aloud. "I'll be going back to England soon."

Anne's husband was in England. Why wasn't she?

"You go, my dear," Anne encouraged her. "Don't let Adam stop you!"

Miranda sighed. "I don't suppose he'll try."

Anne smiled a wistful smile. "He'll try. All women are toys to him and he doesn't consider them capable of having lives of their own, not if he happens to want them at that moment. It's different, of course, once he's tired of the game. Then she's left on her own to pick up the scattered pieces of what was once her life. I know all about Adam from first-hand experience!"

Was Adam the reason Anne Forster and her husband lived apart? Miranda was sure it was. Her imagination was only too ready to supply a picture of Anne locked in Adam's arms, for, somehow, she had known from the very beginning they had once been lovers, and Mr. Forster, discovering them together, had gone off on his own back to England.

"Why do you go on living here?" she asked.

"It's my home," Anne said simply. "Why should I leave?"

Miranda regarded her unhappy face in silence. She could understand the other woman's reluctance to leave. She had only spent one night here, but already it would be a wrench to her when she knew she would not be coming back again.

"Did you live here always?" she asked Anne.

"No."

Miranda was surprised. "I thought you were born and brought up here," she said.

"Only since my marriage. As a child I lived in Colombo. Adam's family and mine were friends since way back. I used to come here for holidays. I always loved this place. When I was a child I used to tell myself how I'd live here when I was grown up."

"In Adam's house?"

"Why not? Adam doesn't appreciate it. I thought Lionel did. Lionel is Adam's step-brother. Did you know that?"

Miranda shook her head. "So you've known him all your life too?"

"He went to school in England. His mother was a very rich woman. Adam was jealous of them both from the moment his father married Lionel's mother. I expect he knew, even then, what all that money would do for the tea plantation. He had always thought it was going to be his, and his alone, instead of the lesser share. He couldn't stand Lionel having anything to do with something he regarded as his, but it was Lionel's mother's money that re-planted the whole estate. Adam may manage the place, but he doesn't own it, not any longer!"

Her note of triumph made Miranda wince. "He owns the house," she said.

"The bungalow? Lionel offered to buy him out but Adam refused. Adam always was a fool about his possessions!"

"Perhaps it was because this was his father's bungalow?"

"And his grandfather's before that! Was that any reason not to share it with Lionel and me?"

"What's mine, remains mine!" Adam's voice said behind them. "And that doesn't only go for houses."

"It's just as well Lionel doesn't think the same way!" Anne retorted with a sad smile. "I've been warning Miranda against your possessive ways!"

"Have you? And what did Miranda have to say?" Adam asked grimly.

"I don't know you well enough to have an opinion," Miranda answered.

The gleam in his eyes could have been caused by the moonlight but she knew it was not. She felt the colour rushing to her cheeks and turned away, wishing she had held her tongue. He put up a hand and pulled on the lobe of her ear, rubbing his forefinger against the soft skin behind. It was a curiously erotic gesture, bringing a weakness to her knees and suspending her breath until it was a painful lump somewhere in her chest.

"Do you have to know me well to have an opinion?"

She pulled away from him. "I bow to Anne's superior knowledge. She's known you far longer!"

"You think that means she knows me better?"

"It must!" Miranda claimed.

He laughed, but there was no amusement that she could detect in the sound. "Anne's knowledge lacks depth. I sometimes wonder if her knowledge of Lionel doesn't also. He seems quite content to stay away!"

"And you know why!" Anne murmured silkily. She pouted up at Adam. "It was more your fault than mine!"

Adam shrugged powerful shoulders. "If it pleases you to think so. Come, Miranda, and I'll show you the garden by moonlight!"

Miranda went with him, but she couldn't help looking back over her shoulder to see Anne sadly drooped over the rail at the edge of the verandah. Perhaps she had wanted to come too?

"No, Miranda."

It was uncanny this ability Adam had to read her mind! Miranda opened her mouth and then shut it again. It wasn't any of her business if he and Anne chose to dwell on old quarrels, she supposed, but she wondered that they could do so and still share the same house. Perhaps they still felt something for each other?

They were out of sight of the house when she next spoke. "It seems everything here isn't subject to Adam after all!"

"In every way that counts," he replied.

"Anne has her independence!"

"Anne belongs to Lionel, not to me."

"And you resent that?"

He was silent for a long moment and she had time to look at the fairyland all about her. The silver light gave the scene an enchantment that sparkled. It was so beautiful it hurt.

"I resent Lionel's weakness, not his possessions," Adam said at last. "If he were a better man he'd have it out with Anne and bring her to heel—"

"Perhaps you made that impossible for him?"

Adam slanted a look at her. "Is that what she told you?"

"I guessed."

"You could be wrong."

"Yes," she admitted, "but I'm not, am I? You and Anne loved each other—"

"Anne never loved anyone, my sweet, not even Lionel."

Miranda waited for him to tell her that he hadn't loved Anne either, but he did nothing of the sort.

"Oh, Adam!" she said at last.

"I don't go for married women. You can't believe the half of what Anne says. She and I were lovers long before she married Lionel, not afterwards."

"But you didn't want to give her up?"

She could feel Adam's anger and wondered why she wasn't afraid of him. His hands grasped her shoulders and he turned her face up to his.

"Anne is not the only pebble on the beach. I've had other women since she married Lionel and I regret nothing! Another man's wife is not what I'm looking for in my bed! Satisfied?"

She tried to avoid looking at him, staring at a space over his shoulder, but what she wanted to do was to slip her arms round his neck and press herself close against him. Then she could no longer resist the temptation to touch the nape of his neck, to feel the short hairs that grew there. "I shouldn't have come," she said, more to herself than to him. "We don't want the same thing—"

"I think we do," he assured her. His expression was almost affectionate, she thought, but it might have been no more than a trick of the moonlight. She didn't think he wasted much time on affection for anyone. He took what he wanted and the devil take the hindmost. She had suspected that from the first time she had seen him, and now Anne had confirmed it.

She shook her head violently. "You only say that because you're not the one who'll get hurt!" she exclaimed angrily.

He gave her a curious look. "Could you be hurt, Miranda?"

She abandoned her pride to the four winds. "Yes," she said.

He took her into his arms and she made no move to resist him. "I'll try not to hurt you," he promised, "but I can't afford to let you go, Miranda."

"Why not?" she questioned him. As if it mattered! For the moment it was enough for her to be held tightly against him, so tightly that she could hardly breathe.

"I want a wife of my own. I want children, *my* children, someone to come after me here—"

"You want to found a dynasty?"

He spread his fingers against her back. "Why not? Soon all this will be mine again and what's the point if there's no one to come after me, to make it live when I am dead and gone?"

"What will it matter to you when you're dead?" she demanded.

"It's mattered to a great many men," he answered dryly. "Why not to me?"

"I don't know," she admitted. "It's a beautiful country, but you're an Englishman. They may not want you here for ever."

"My family has lived here for generations—"

"How many generations?"

"More than a hundred years. I think of myself as Lankan, not as English, and I hope my children will do the same."

"Wouldn't it be better if they had a Lankan mother?"

"I have other qualities in mind for their mother, qualities that you have in abundance, fair Miranda. Won't you stay in paradise and marry me?"

"No, I couldn't! I'm not even sure I want to have children! I want to be married for myself alone, not as a brood-mare. You should have married Anne because she wants to live here too, and would do anything to live in your house—"

"And you won't?"

"Not I!"

She thought how large and solid he looked and wondered she had found the courage to defy him. But to be married for those reasons? She couldn't bear it! She wanted to be the love of his life, more precious to him than anything else on earth, not someone possessing the right qualities to be the mother of his children! Any woman would do for that!

"I won't let you go," he warned her.

"You can't keep me here against my will!"

His eyes gleamed dangerously. "But will it be against your will? You may fight a bit at the start, but you won't hold out against me for long."

She drew herself up, her head held high. "I'll hold out as long as necessary. You think too much of yourself, Adam Ferguson!"

"Do I?" he mocked her. "Do I indeed?"

"I won't marry you!" She wished she sounded more confident. Her voice trembled in the most despicable way and she was shocked to discover that the very real fear she was feeling was also pleasurable to her. Her every sense was sharpened by the anticipation of what he might do next.

"If you don't I'll take you without marriage!" he retorted.

"You'll do nothing of the sort!"

"Then you'd better agree to marry me quickly. The choice is yours!"

"I think I'll go back to the house," she said with dignity. "We've left Anne on her own for long enough."

"Good idea, but I think you may find Anne has already gone to bed. It's later than you think!"

Her heart pounded and she could feel the beat of it in the back of her throat. "Adam, find someone else—"

"I found you!"

"No, no, I can't let you! Please let me go!"

He caught her by the wrists, pulling her off-balance against him. His hands went to her waist and he lifted her easily, throwing her over his shoulder. She pounded on his back with clenched fists and kicked out with her legs, but his hold was too firm for her to break free.

"Where are you taking me?" she demanded angrily.

"To bed. Where else?"

Miranda had always thought of herself as a strong girl, but now, wriggle as she might, she knew she could not win free. She forced herself to go limp and, obligingly, his arm relaxed about her hips. In a second she had brought her knee up against his chest and pushed away from him with her hands. She fell heavily onto the damp ground and was on her feet in a flash.

"Don't come near me!" she dared him.

His laughter jarred on her ears. "I mean to come a great deal nearer, my dear Miranda. Have you hurt yourself?"

"No!"

She wasn't sure whether she was denying the first or the second part of his speech. The fall had knocked the breath out of her and her frustrated feelings did nothing for her temper.

He bent down and picked her up bodily once again, swinging her off her feet and into his arms. "It would serve you right if you were hurt! Give up, Miranda, and accept your fate."

"I don't believe in fate!"

It was unfair that he could carry her so easily and so far. He showed no sign of any discomfort from her weight, which was that of any healthy girl of her height. She put her arms round his neck to lessen the burden, knowing herself to be a traitor to her own interests as she did so.

She refused to answer. When he came closer she opened her mouth to bite him and she would have done too, but, somehow, he seemed to know exactly what she intended and his lips fastened themselves on hers, his tongue probing the sweetness of her mouth. She fought every inch of the way but, in the end, it was her own body which betrayed her. Already roused by his kisses, when he placed his hands on her breasts her struggles became an enticement for him to explore further, as she herself was doing to him.

It was he who drew back. He stood beside the bed, caressing her cheek with a thoughtful finger.

"Marry me, Miranda," he said at last, "and make my dreams come true!"

She didn't want to talk. Nor did she want him to leave her now. "Adam?" she murmured. "Adam, where are you going?"

"Nowhere!"

He switched off the light and came back to the bed, doffing his sarong as he came. "Where did you think I was going?"

She put an arm up over her face. "I thought you'd changed your mind."

"Only if you say you'll marry me?"

"And what if we don't have any sons? We're all girls in my family."

He touched her shoulder and then her breast. "You have sisters?"

"No, I'm the only one. But my cousins are all girls."

She reached out a hand and buried her fingers in the hairs on his chest. She could feel his heart-beat, slow, deliberate and un-moved, and wondered what it would take to excite him as he was exciting her.

"It's the man who determines the sex of the child," he told her. "I would have only myself to blame."

"No!" she said again. "I won't marry you! For marriage one needs love and liking—"

"Shall I make you love me, Miranda?"

"You can't make me like you!"

"I'll settle for a wife to warm my bed and bear my children. You'll never want for anything as my wife—"

"Not even your love?"

"I want you, more than I've ever wanted any other woman. I want to make love to you now, and you want me to, don't you, Miranda?"

She turned to face him, the tears running down her cheeks. "Yes," she said, the word wrung out of her as if it were an agony to her. "I wanted you the first moment I saw you in that crowd!"

"And you'll marry me?"

She moved closer against him. "Yes, I'll marry you," she sighed. "I'll probably regret it, but I'll marry you whenever you say. Only, be kind to me,

Adam, because there won't be anyone else. There'll only be you and a strange land—and Anne Forster."

He kissed her hard on the lips. "A woman has no need of anyone else but her husband," he assured her. "She's a part of him. Adam's rib!"

And how long would that last? she wondered.

Chapter Six

Miranda had not wanted to sleep by herself. She remembered with a dull sense of humiliation that she had pleaded with Adam to stay with her but he had gone just the same. He had known very well how to rouse her, but he had seemed perfectly calm and unfeeling himself, as she had discovered when she had put her hand on his chest and had felt the slow, unhurried beat of his heart.

What kind of a marriage was it going to be? It was bound to be disastrous as far as she was concerned for she wanted much more out of life than to be the mother of a parcel of children. She wanted love—Adam's love!—because it was Adam she had fallen in love with. She hadn't wanted to fall in love with him, she had seen the dangers from the start, and she wasn't sure she even liked him very much, but she loved him with an aching longing that refused to go away and which only he could assuage.

His bedroom was a delight to her. It was a large room, with french-windows leading straight out into the garden. The furniture had been kept to a minimum; the bed she was lying on, a chest of drawers, and a couple of tables. A built-in cupboard held most of his clothes and the door balanced the one leading into the private bathroom that was apparently one of the few luxuries he allowed himself in his own home. All the furniture was made of hard-wood, carved and decorated with designs that she concluded were to do with local religious motifs. The floor was made from blocks of the same wood, covered with a few oriental style rugs that she thought might have been brought over from India. There were few ornaments, a picture or two, one of women washing themselves in brightly coloured saris, and one which was a batik wall-hanging, also of women though this time with bowls of fruit and flowers on their heads. Adam, she thought, had an eye for women, and that was hardly likely to change after marriage to her either.

She rolled over and looked at the watch on her wrist. It was late, nearly eight o'clock. She was never going to get to the hotel in Kandy in time to start work. She sighed heavily. She was not looking forward to the explanations she was going to have to make to Liam O'Grady and the others. They would think her mad! Nor would they want to leave her behind when they went back to England. She would ask Liam to call on her mother and reassure her, for her mother liked Liam, but first he would need some kind of explanation himself and Miranda had none to offer him.

"Is my lady taking breakfast this morning?"

She started, very conscious of her naked state. "I didn't hear you knock!" she said to her tormentor.

Adam smiled amiably. "I seldom knock in my own house." His eyes glinted wickedly. "What have you got to hide, Miranda?"

From him, very little, she reflected gloomily. "Everyone has a right to some privacy," she rebuked him.

"You'll have to get used to my being around. I like looking at you," he said simply.

"Not before breakfast surely?"

He laughed. "Especially before breakfast! You have a lovely, creamy skin that looks like pure silk in daylight. Why should I deny myself?"

She blushed. "Consideration for other people's feelings?" she suggested.

He put the tray he was carrying down on one of the tables and came over to the bed. "I consider you all the time," he said. He studied her face, putting a hand under her chin so that she couldn't escape his searching look. "Did you sleep at all?" he asked her.

"Not much," she confessed. She looked down her nose, anything rather than look at him with his clean-cut newly shaved face and his all-seeing light-grey eyes. "I didn't feel much like sleep."

His mouth tightened. "Perhaps I should have stayed and given you something else to think about."

"But you didn't want to stay! I can't think why you want to marry me—yes, I can, because you want a son to come after you! But why *me*?"

"You're here, and you're a highly desirable

woman. It'll be many a night before I tire of having you in my bed!"

"I see," she said, but all she saw was that love didn't come into it.

"I wonder if you do," he murmured. "You won't regret marrying me, Miranda, I promise you that."

"How can you know?" she demanded.

"Your happiness will be in my hands. Don't you think I'm able to make a woman happy?"

She would have had no doubt about it, on a short-term basis, but it was his love she wanted. "I may fall in love with someone else," she said, hurting herself as much as she hoped to hurt him. "What will you do then?"

"Unlikely," he said briefly. "I shall keep you far too busy for that!" He sounded amused.

"And what about you?" she retorted, stung.

"My wife will be the centre of my home, but what I do away from home is none of your business. Forget your doubts, Miranda, and be happy! There are a great many advantages on your side too, you know. You'll be financially secure, in a home you already like with a husband who attracts you physically and who certainly won't be neglecting you. The more I see you the more I want you. You weren't the only one to spend a sleepless night last night."

Miranda thought about reminding him that it was not her fault that he had left her to spend the night on her own, but the idea of reminding him how she had pleaded with him to stay with her was humiliating to her. She had thought she had too much strength of mind to plead with any man and yet, with

Adam, he had only to lay a hand on her and she melted. Well, she must banish these thoughts from her brain and think about her career.

"I'm late for work," she said finally.

"They're not expecting you to work today. I telephoned your manager to tell him your news. He wants to make sure you're doing the right thing and he's coming out here to see you this afternoon." His eyes narrowed. "He seemed unnecessarily concerned about you. I suppose he is your manager and nothing more?"

"I've known him for a long time," Miranda explained.

"And he's not above making a pass, or stealing a kiss?"

"He has kissed me, yes," Miranda said with dignity. "My mother likes him. She would have been very happy if we had had a closer relationship—"

"He'd better keep his hands off you from now on!" Adam growled.

"And if he doesn't?" she challenged.

He put his hands round her neck, exerting only the faintest pressure, but leaving her in no doubt that if he had a mind to, the punishment he dealt out could be severe.

"My sons are going to be fathered by me and not by any other man!"

Miranda steeled herself to face him without flinching. "Unless you keep on the right side of me you'll never be sure of that!" she said boldly.

His fingers relaxed. "Oh, Miranda, what an innocent you are!" He bent down and kissed her on the lips. "I can read you like a book and no other man will do for you!"

He pulled the covering sheet away from her, his fingers finding and caressing her breast. Her hand covered his, but only to hold it more closely against her.

"It isn't fair!" she exclaimed.

He smiled at the agitated rise and fall of her silky-smooth flesh. "Shall I make you fall in love with me, Miranda?" he asked her softly.

Her sharp intake of breath brought a cruel twist to his lips. "You're trembling on the brink now, my beautiful one, and it would be one way of putting Liam O'Grady out of your heart and mind—for ever!"

"You sound as if you think love is a weakness!" she snapped at him.

" I do."

She pushed him away, making to get up. "I don't understand you at all!" she said crossly. "I suppose some woman gave you the run-around once and now you think we're all tarred with the same brush! It doesn't say much for your intelligence!"

He sat down on the bed, watching her out of lazy eyes. "I'm willing to be converted to another point of view, but women are best kept in their proper place. They get strident when they think they're in command."

"Indeed?" She suspected he was teasing her. "Was your mother ever strident?"

"My step-mother was."

Miranda was appalled by the bitterness in his

voice. "It was her money that saved the estate, wasn't it?"

"We would have gotten by without it. My father, however, was unable to say no to her about anything. He gave away his heritage—and mine!—for the sake of a quiet life. That's not a mistake I shall ever make!"

Miranda shivered. "Why does it matter so much to you whose money it was?" she asked curiously. "Your step-brother doesn't seem to interfere in its running and the house is still yours."

He sat up straight, regarding her with brooding eyes. "He doesn't interfere for the very good reason that the men won't work for him. He and Anne thought this place was a toy to play with, but they found they couldn't manage without me. Labor may be cheap, but it won't be for long with the government breathing down the back of our necks. And a good thing too! Your countrymen are going to have to learn to pay the price for their beloved tea. Men and women's lives go into producing it; never forget it. My revered brother didn't see it that way. He would have cut the workers' pitiful wages down to the bone and then some! Bad luck to him!"

Miranda found her clothes and began to dress. She would have preferred to have the room to herself, but she hadn't the strength for another battle of wills with Adam quite yet. Besides, he was not looking at her but was sitting on the edge of the bed darkly brooding over the tea estate.

"How did you make him change his mind?" she prompted him.

"There was a lot of international pressure on the government. The rich always expect more from the poor than they will attempt themselves. Quite where they thought Sri Lanka was to get the money to make the changes they thought desirable, nobody knows. Many of our Tamil workers retain their Indian nationality and send a proportion of their wages to their families over there who are even poorer than they are themselves. But the government does what it can, and Lionel is not a citizen of the island which made it easier for them. He couldn't do anything right by the time they had finished with him!"

When she had dressed she stood before him. He lifted his head and she caught the quizzical gleam at the back of his light-grey eyes and felt her cheeks grow hot.

"Very pretty!" he commended her. "But I prefer you as I first saw you this morning. What's more I like to think I'm the first man who has ever seen you that way?"

"You know you are!" she flared, turning away to the breakfast tray.

When she held up the tea-pot, she was annoyed to find her hands were trembling. "Have you had breakfast?" she asked.

"A couple of hours ago. I'll have a cup of tea with you though. If you want more than the fruit and rolls I brought you, you have only to ring the bell and Sita will bring you bacon and eggs."

She picked up a slice of pineapple and put it on a

plate. "This fruit is all I need. It's more than I usually have for breakfast, but I can't resist it. Does it go on all the year round?"

"It does." He took her fork from her and helped himself to a bite of her pineapple. "Does that reconcile you to living in paradise?"

She blinked at him. "It may come from the forbidden Tree of Knowledge."

"We don't have apples here."

"It may have been a peach or a nectarine," she argued. "The Bible doesn't say it was an apple."

He took another piece of her fruit. "Eat away, my Eve! It was after they had eaten the forbidden fruit that Adam and Eve knew each other. And I never heard that Adam regretted giving way to temptation." He grinned wickedly at Miranda.

"They certainly lived together for a long, long time," she said, determinedly ignoring the insinuation. *Despite his other women.*

Adam looked surprised. "Were there any?"

"There was Lilith—if the legends are to be believed. Perhaps she was the serpent who inhabited Eden, jealous of his rejection of her.

Adam's expression was enigmatic. "Who have you cast as Lilith?" he asked with sardonic mockery.

"You know who!" she retorted.

"So I do," he admitted almost casually. "Now there's a woman better dressed than undressed, quite the opposite of present company."

Miranda tried not to look as shaken as she felt. There was something that she had to know, but she couldn't find the words to ask him. He would laugh at her and twist her meaning, but it was important to her, more important than anything else had ever been.

"Is that how you see me?" she managed at last. "As a body rather than a person? Don't you care what I *think* at all?"

"Not a lot," he admitted cheerfully. Then seeing her crestfallen expression he went on, "My dear Miranda, I know what you think without having to be told."

"You know some of the things I think, but you don't know me at all," she said. "Sometimes I don't even know myself."

He was amused by that. "Drink your tea, Miranda. If you go on looking so miserable I may be tempted to kiss it better and it wouldn't stop there. You wouldn't want me to anticipate our marriage would you?"

She shook her head, then took a sip of tea, and then another, allowing the smooth liquid to soothe away the lump in the back of her throat. She was used to drinking tea from tea-bags straight from the supermarket, but this was something very different. This was delicious! A golden amber drink, with none of the bitter aftertaste of the cheap teas. This required neither milk nor lemon to make it palatable.

"We don't get tea like this. in England!" she exclaimed.

"No, we keep that back for ourselves. We don't pick enough to make it worthwhile commercially. I'll get Anne to show you over the factory, if you're interested?"

Miranda would rather have had Adam as a guide but she didn't like to say so. Besides, she thought, if she and Anne were going to live in the same house for any time, the sooner they got to know each other the better.

"Are you sure they're not expecting me at the hotel?"

"Not until tomorrow. Liam O'Grady will take you back with him tonight. As soon as you've finished your assignment we'll be married."

Her stomach turned over at the thought. "Where?" she asked blankly.

"Where else but here in your future home?" He took her cup from her and placed it on the tray, picking up the remains of their breakfast in an easy movement. "Anne will be waiting for you on the verandah." His eyes met hers, and his were stern and as hard as stone. "Don't let her make trouble between us, Miranda. It will be your fault if she does!"

Miranda sat on the edge of the bed, her head in her hands, for a long time after he had gone. She tried telling herself it didn't matter what she did, except to her, but she couldn't entirely dismiss how her mother would feel about this strange marriage. Miranda's father had died when she was still a child and she and her mother had always been close, there being just the two of them. She knew how her mother had planned to see her married in the church where they had worshipped all her life. The church was all that remained of an old abbey, the rest of it having been pulled down as being far too large for the population of the tiny East Sussex town. Once, long ago, there had been a terrible storm in the night, and the river, which had entered the sea somewhere near New Romney in Kent, had moved its course into Sussex. On that night Old Winchelsea had fallen into the sea, and some people said to this very day that when the seas were high you could hear the bells of the church tolling beneath the waves.

Winchelsea had been re-built, one of the very first towns to be planned on the grid system, with the new abbey in a square in the middle. That had been way back in the Middle Ages, and nothing much had happened to Winchelsea since. It was a pretty town though, with well-spaced houses, almost all of them built in by-gone centuries, and a rather handsome town-wall, near one of the towers of which stood her mother's house, English and picturesque, with roses growing at the door. She would never understand how her daughter could get married without her, let alone in a foreign country and with such unseemly haste. Mrs. Wade would be unbearably hurt that she had known nothing about it. But there seemed nothing Miranda could do about it.

Anne was sitting in a garden-chair on the verandah. Neat in all her movements, she perched on the edge of the chair, her legs crossed in front of her and her hands folded in her lap. She was watching some birds, flirting as they crossed and recrossed the slopes of the lawn. They were of a pretty green colour, brilliant exploding jewels as their feathers caught the sun.

"You fool!" she greeted Miranda without so much

as moving her head. "Adam certainly has you where he wants you!"

Miranda sat down beside her. "What if he has?"

"Don't you think any other woman wouldn't serve his purpose just as well?"

"Yes, I think she probably could," Miranda admitted.

"Then where's your pride? You could at least give him a run for his money instead of falling into his arms as soon as look at him!"

Miranda wished she were older and very much wiser. "I don't think that's any business of yours," she said quietly.

Anne looked at her then, her mouth quivering and her blue eyes filled with unshed tears. "He's wanted to punish me for a long, long time and now you've given him the means to do it. He wouldn't have looked at you otherwise! We have our own traditions here and you're not part of them! Why don't you go back to England to where you belong?"

"Why don't you join your husband in England?" Miranda countered.

Anne laughed harshly. "My husband! He should be here, making something of his inheritance if he were any kind of a man, not leaving it to Adam to make a monkey of him! I could have had Adam once . . . but I didn't want a poor man . . . and Adam was poor then. I guess I just made the wrong choice."

Miranda had never seen anyone cry who did it as beautifully as did Anne Forster. The tears trickled down her cheeks, but her eyes never changed colour and there wasn't the remotest sign of puffiness to their lids.

Anne smiled her sad smile and wiped her cheeks with her fingers. "Adam was my lover before I married Lionel. I am hoping he will be again. Marry him if you must, Miss Wade, but it won't last. Adam has always been mine, and once he's successfully ousted Lionel I shall want him back. Don't say you haven't been warned!"

Miranda thought she had known it all along. She tried to pretend it made no difference to her having it spelt out in words by this woman she disliked increasingly every time she saw her, but it was an added barrier between herself and Adam. If only she could believe that he loved her. But he had never told her so. Had he ever told Anne he loved her? Did he still?

"Adam said you'd show me the tea-factory," she said aloud in level tones. "The tea I had for breakfast was absolutely delicious and I'd love to know something about how it's produced."

Anne smiled again. "Quite the proprietress, aren't you? I suppose you'll be giving me orders to pack my bags soon? But Adam won't allow it. *You* won't have any say in how you live here, not if you live here a hundred years!"

"So Adam tells me," Miranda agreed dryly.

"And you agreed to his making all the decisions?"

"I agreed to marry him."

Anne's eyes flickered over Miranda's tense face. "What a quaint, old-fashioned little thing you are! I can see why he chose you! You'll make him a story-book wife, warming his slippers and feeding him his favourite meals when he comes in tired after a long day. My dear, you'll bore him stiff in a week!"

Adam had put it at a little longer than that, but he too had known he would want more than Miranda had to offer in the end. Miranda felt sick at the thought. Was it asking so much to want to be the only woman in his life and in his heart?

"Then I'd better make the most of the time I have and enjoy it while I can," Miranda said, lifting her chin.

Anne pursed up her mouth, a shocked look on her face. "There is a great deal of the animal in Adam. I hope you haven't mistaken a momentary attraction for something deeper."

"If Adam's an animal, he's a very splendid one," Miranda said dreamily before she could stop herself. "Is Lionel like him?"

"No, he is not!" Anne bit off the words angrily. "Lionel is a civilised human being such as I am myself. He seldom bothered me even when we were first married. He respects women as being something more than the answer to his physical needs! He's not at all like Adam!"

She rose to her feet, her mouth pulled into a tight line. "If you want to look round the factory we'd better go there now. Adam says you have a friend coming this afternoon? You probably don't want to get back too late."

They walked to the end of the garden that looked out onto cloud-capped mountains and deep craggy valleys filled with the sound of falling water. Mile upon mile of the contour-planted tea bushes stretched away as far as the eye could see. Miranda filled her lungs with the pure, mentholated air, marvelling at the brilliant sunshine which lit up the scene before her.

"I'm not surprised Adam never wants to leave here!" she exclaimed.

Anne shrugged her shoulders indifferently. "The best teas have to be grown up here. They need the sunshine, the cold nights, and the mists that cling in the valleys and which retard the growth but give the leaf its aromatic flavour. Further down one gets a greater 'flush' of leaf, but they can only be used as fillers in the blends you buy at home. Connoisseurs can tell which glen the tea has been grown in, just like Scotch whiskey. Mutations in flavour and the liquoring properties, as they call it, change with altitude, soil, rainfall, and hours of sunshine. It's a complicated business."

The factory fascinated Miranda. It was here the green leaf was cured into black tea. She watched it being dessicated and coming out of the drying racks looking like pieces of green silk, and followed it along the rollers that broke it up to release the aromatic juices, from where it went on to be fermented, when the colour change from green to a bright copper was completed. After that it was "fired" to prevent any further oxidisation by baking the tea evenly.

Reduced to a quarter of its original size and weight, the tea was then sorted and graded by size into leaf and broken grades, fannings and dust, and by quality into categories with names like Orange Pekoe, Pekoe Souchong, Tippy, and Flowery.

Nor did it end there, for the tea had to be tasted and labelled in the jargon of the trade as malty, pointy, bakey, thick, coppery, dull, or bright, according to flavour and how well it infused when hot water was added. The tasters never swallowed the tea, but swilled it round their mouth and over their tongue, spitting out the liquid again.

"Want to try?" Anne asked her languidly, bored by the whole proceedings.

Miranda nodded and the taster brewed a whole new batch of teas for her to sample and let her guess which were the best and which the less good teas. Some of them were easy to detect, but others seemed to her inexperienced palate to be identical to each other. Once she thought she detected a change of colour and earned the taster's earnest commendation for her powers of observation.

He didn't offer any of the teas to Anne. Indeed, he seemed to be ill at ease in her presence and Miranda wondered why. She liked the man and could guess how valuable was his gift to Adam. There couldn't be many men whose sense of taste was so finely developed.

A telephone bell went by the man's desk and he excused himself to answer it.

"He doesn't like me," Anne volunteered, jerking the words out. "Lionel tried to get rid of him. He made a pass at me—"

She broke off as the man came back, smiling at

Miranda. "It's Mr. Ferguson. He says will you please go back to the house because he is expecting a call from your mother. Will you please hurry, Miss Wade." His smile grew wider. "A telephone call from England! It's a long, long way for a call to come!"

[faint show-through text, illegible]

Chapter Seven

"Mama? How did you know I was here?"

Her mother's voice came to her as clearly as if she were in the next room. "Adam rang me last night. Are you very happy, darling?"

Miranda wondered if she were. "I don't know," she confessed.

"I know the feeling," her mother consoled her. "I felt exactly the same when I became engaged to your father. I didn't know if I were on my head or my heels. But I like him, Miranda. I like him very much. I think you've chosen well. He's asked me out to see you later on—when I've found someone to look after the dog and the cats, and the house too, come to that. I'm sorry I won't see you married, love, but as long as I know it's to a good man—"

"Adam isn't a good man!"

Mrs. Wade laughed comfortably. "Swept you off

your feet, has he? You don't know what to make of it?"

"No, Mama, I didn't mean that. I meant that I don't know if I want to marry him at all. He's bossy and pig-headed, and he has to have his own way about everything! I should be working now!"

"You work too hard; I've thought so for some time. I'm glad he means to look after you. We had a nice chat last night and I refuse to worry about you, Miranda. It won't do you any harm to be ordered about a bit now. I never did enough of that—you were always as much my friend as my daughter—but Adam—"

"I always thought you liked Liam O'Grady?" Miranda wailed.

"I do, but he doesn't compare with Adam Ferguson! Adam has the same strength of character that your father had. I could tell it at once! And whatever he may say to you, you must admit he has your welfare at heart, telephoning to me last night and accepting the charges for this call too. Darling, if you ask me, you're a lucky girl!"

"But I don't want to live the rest of my life subject to Adam!"

Mrs. Wade refused to be impressed. "Think of the alternative," she advised, laughing again. "Think of *not* living with Adam!"

It was indeed a sobering thought. Now that Adam had stirred her senses and awoken her to the possibilities of passion, she could never be quite the same person again. She would have her career, it was true, but that could never be her whole life as it had been before. She wanted other things now. She wanted Adam.

"I am thinking," she said. "But you don't know all the circumstances. Still I'm glad you called. I wish you were here, Mama!"

"You'll manage very well without me!" her mother assured her dryly. "Adam must come first with you now."

Miranda stood in the hall by the phone a long time after she had replaced the receiver. She felt, in an odd way, as though a chasm had opened up before her feet. Her mother had been her last excuse as to why she shouldn't marry Adam and now he had taken that away from her. How he had managed to persuade Mrs. Wade that he was the ideal man for her daughter over the telephone was beyond Miranda. It wasn't even as though her mother *liked* the telephone! So why had she been so delighted with Adam? What was there about him to convince her that Miranda could do no better than to surrender her life and her future into the hands of a man who was a stranger to them both?

Adam found her there. He regarded her with a quizzical expression and a slight lift of his eyebrows.

"Feeling better?"

She shook her head. "I think you're some sort of devil!" she burst out.

The nice thing about Adam was that he never had to ask what all the fuss was. He knew exactly what she was talking about.

"I had a feeling you might be close to your mother," was all he said.

"So you subverted her to your own ends?"

"If I did, it wasn't deliberate. I wanted her on my side, but only because I thought it would make you happier if you knew she wasn't worrying about you."

"Well, yes," she said, "but I thought she wanted me to marry someone else!"

"Liam O'Grady?"

She coloured, refusing to answer. "She's more easily influenced by masculine charm than I thought. She mistakes it for strength of character!"

His smile mocked her. "Like mother, like daughter?"

"Oh I'm undecided on the point!" she claimed. "I know you're dangerous when crossed, but I don't think that shows much strength of character. On the contrary, a mature person wouldn't mind losing every now and again!"

"I'll bear it in mind," he said. "As long as I win the points that matter between us." He put an arm about her waist, his hand sliding down to her hip. She longed to fling herself into his arms, but of course she couldn't do that. All she had left was her self-respect, and that was a poor, battered thing since she had pleaded with him to stay with her the night before.

"I don't like being pawed!" she said sharply.

He gave her a squeeze with his hand and let her go. "For now! But don't push me too far, Miranda my sweet. This is a difficult time for us both."

She couldn't see that it was a difficult time for him at all. "I wish Liam would come," she said. "I feel guilty not turning up for work this morning as I said I would."

"Would you like to come into Kandy with me?"

Her face cleared as if by magic. "May I?"

"I'll take you to lunch. The dancers will be practising for tonight and you can watch them while I transact my business at the bank. Afterwards we'll have a truly Ceylonese meal, finishing up with the ginger tea that all the village people drink. How will that suit?"

"On our own?" she asked him cautiously.

"I wasn't thinking of taking anyone else," he answered.

"Oh good!"

"Anne doesn't like ginger tea," he told her soberly. "Most Europeans don't. I guess it's an acquired taste."

Miranda put a tentative hand on his arm. "May we go and see the botanical gardens sometime? I've read about the orchids they have there, and the ebony trees, and the tree the Queen planted when she was here. If you don't have time today, I'd like to see them before I go back to England—"

She broke off at the expression on his face.

"I shall hold you to your promise to marry me, Miranda, come what may!" he scowled.

She wiped her damp palms on her trousered thighs. "I'd forgotten for the moment," she tried to explain. "But, Adam, it might be better if I did go back to England, better for both of us!"

His hands fastened on her shoulders. They hurt, but he showed no signs of noticing her wincing away from him. "You're staying here. Give up any idea of going back to England with Liam O'Grady or anyone else! You're mine, and here is where you belong!"

"All right!" she cried out, but it wasn't what she wanted to say. Deep in her heart she was still asking why he should want her when he didn't love her, when any reasonably attractive girl would do?

Miranda forgot her troubles as she sat beside Adam in the Landrover. The countryside was a constant delight to her, especially when they rounded a corner and there, in the middle of nowhere, was a scarlet painted letter-box, exactly like the ones back home, even to the cypher of the then-reigning monarch on its door, though she couldn't catch which one it had been as they hurtled past.

Kandy was somnolent in the heat of the mid-day sun. The streets were decorated for the evening processions, and those who were strolling about on the pavements were mostly in their best clothes of brightly coloured saris, or the unisex sarong, which both men and women tied about their lower bodies, shifting them and retying them every few minutes as they moved about.

Perhaps because it was the time of the processions in honour of the Sacred Tooth there were still a great many devotees crowded round the temple. Adam glanced at his watch.

"Do you want to have a look inside?" he asked her.

Miranda nodded silently. She had no idea what to expect, but she was struck by the gentle, smiling faces of the never ending stream of people bearing their offerings up the steps that led to the main doors. They carried pink lotus blossoms and white frangipanni, the temple flower that is frequently grown near every temple so that even the poorest visitor to the shrine might pick the flowers and have something to offer. Their scent mingled with the perfume of joss-sticks and dust and the sandalwood soap used by many of the women. Adam and Miranda left their shoes outside with the others.

Inside, the noise of the drummers was deafening. They stood in a semi-circle, their whole bodies shaking in time to the beat, their turbans tossing with the effort and the sweat pouring down their naked chests to their scarlet cummerbunds. All around them people drifted hither and thither, busy about their devotions.

It seemed dark inside at first after the sunshine outside. Miranda stood, blinking, very close to Adam, suddenly afraid that she might lose him in the melee all about them. He drew her hand through his arm and smiled down at her.

"It's a bit overpowering at first, isn't it?" he said. "Let's go upstairs and see where the relic is kept." He kept a light hold on her wrist as they mounted the ancient, stone steps.

It was here that most people had come to make their offerings. The stairs were crowded with silent, marvellously poised men, women and children, waiting their turn to pass before the Sacred Tooth of the Lord Buddha, even though it was not now on display.

When they finally passed by the door, lowering their heads in silent respect, Adam began to tell her how the Japanese Buddhists had given the crystal display case, and where many of the other objects had come from, but Miranda found it hard to take it all in.

They came down another flight of stairs and went back outside to retrieve their shoes.

"I hate to tell you," said Adam, "but they never take the Tooth outside the Temple these days. It's thought it would bring bad luck if they did. The elephant carried a replica reliquary round the streets."

It was another illusion gone. "But everyone was so devoted!" she exclaimed. "They paid it so much honour! Don't they know it's not there?"

"It doesn't have to be there for them to pay it honour. The merit gained is gained by performing in the procession, by dancing or drumming—"

"Or riding Nellie?"

A muscle jerked in his cheek. "I hope so. It brought me you."

Miranda looked at him. *She had to know.* "Did you know Anne is thinking of divorcing Lionel?" she burst out.

Adam's lips twisted. "Did she tell you so?"

"Not in so many words, no, but that was what she meant. It was what you wanted at one time, wasn't it?"

When he didn't answer, Miranda sat down on the stone steps and put her shoes on. She didn't want to look at him while he was thinking about Anne! When he spoke to Lionel's wife his eyes weren't as cold as ice, but were as warm and lively as the lake beside the Temple.

He left her sitting by the lake while he went to the

bank. Some women came close by, laughing together as they tried to persuade their toddlers to walk by themselves for a few steps. She watched them idly. Would she ever have children? *Adam's children.* She shivered in anticipation.

"Well, well, fancy meeting you here!"

Miranda started, and turned to meet the smiling face of Liam O'Grady.

"Liam!"

"You may well look guilty," he rebuked her. "I thought you were too tired to work today?"

"Is that what Adam told you?"

"He did, if Adam is that forceful gentleman who has taken over your life these last two days?"

"More than that," she sighed, "he plans to take over for life!"

"Your mother won't like that," he warned her.

"But she does! She's very happy about it!"

Liam swore under his breath. "And how do you feel about it? It isn't like you, Miranda, to upset all our working schedules like this! I didn't get you this assignment for you to play the fool as soon as you get far enough away from home! I thought you took your work seriously?"

"I do!" she protested. "I always have! But Adam—"

"Can't you say no to him?"

She shook her head humbly, looking young and defenceless. "He walked into my life and he won't walk out again."

"Are you trying to tell me he fell for you on sight?"

Miranda bit her lip. How simple everything would

be if he had! "No. Oh, it's so difficult to explain—especially to you!"

"Try me," Liam invited her.

"I don't want to hurt you," Miranda admitted.

"I can look after myself. Can you?"

"Probably not!" she said on a mirthless laugh. "I haven't many defences against Adam, and he knows it."

"The chemistry is right?"

She nodded. "Very right. He says now, though, he doesn't think it'll last. What'll I do if it doesn't?"

Liam stared out across the lake. "Come home to me," he suggested after a pause. "There'll always be a welcome on the mat for you at my place!"

But she shook her head, swallowing down the tears that came uninvited into the back of her throat. "I won't do that. It wouldn't be fair to you. But thanks for the offer!"

Liam gave her a sad look. "Shall I speak to Ferguson for you?"

Miranda went cold at the thought. She veiled her eyes with her lashes to hide the panic she knew would be revealed in them.

"I think it's better to leave things alone," she said, her voice a thin thread in her throat.

"I can't if you're going to take days off without warning and throw out all our schedules. You do realise that, don't you, darling?"

She nodded unhappily. "It won't happen again," she promised.

"I wish I could be sure of that. What are your plans, Miranda?"

She shrugged her shoulders, feeling a fool, because she couldn't even tell him that. She had no idea what Adam was planning for her, except that he meant to keep her in Sri Lanka when the others went home.

"Adam and I are going to get married—"

"When?"

"When I've finished my assignment with you."

"You're not coming back to England with us?"

She licked her lips, frozen with fear. "I wish I could! Liam, don't tell the airline, or *anybody,* that I'm not coming! I may not be able to stay after all. Something may happen to prevent it, and I wouldn't want *not* to be able to get home!"

Liam leaned forward, picked up a pebble and set it skidding across the water. "It sounds to me as though you're in a proper mess, my girl. I can't help thinking you'd feel better if you told your Uncle Liam all about it."

"I can't now!" she jerked out. "I'm having lunch with Adam. He's gone to the bank, but he'll be back any time now."

Liam frowned. "Are you frightened of Adam Ferguson?" he asked.

"I don't think so, but I don't know anything any more!" she confessed. "I don't know why he should want to marry me even!"

"Could it be that suitable girls don't come two-a-penny over here?" Liam suggested cruelly.

"I don't think Adam would be short of suitable women if he lived on a desert island!" Miranda retorted, trying not to sound bitter. "They'd swim across oceans to get to him!"

Liam stared at her. "You're in love with him!" he accused.

"He's not in love with me," she said flatly. "He says he wants to make love to me, but he can wait until we're married. I think that is only a passing attraction." She realised, too late, the unsuitability of discussing such things with Liam O'Grady, and her face burned with shame. She put an anxious hand on his thigh, not noticing at all how he pulled away from her touch. "Please forget I said that, Liam," she pleaded with him. "I shouldn't have said it. I wouldn't have done if I hadn't been confused and unsure of myself. I expect most newly engaged girls feel just the same, only I seem to be making more of a meal of it than they do! I had no business to burden you with my troubles."

"I'm an old friend. Doesn't that give me some rights?" he questioned her, as unhappy as she.

"No, and you know why not. I haven't played fair with you, and I'm sorry. You'd do far better to forget all about me!"

"Easier said than done!" he grunted.

Only a week ago Miranda would have told him it was no more than a matter of will-power and a sensible attitude to what one could and couldn't have. She thought uneasily that whatever else Adam had done for her, he had caused her to grow up in the last two days. She had been a child when she had come to Sri Lanka, but whatever happened to her now, she would never be that same child again. Her lips trembled as she remembered her own inability to bear the thought of life without Adam, and she could only hope that Liam didn't feel the same way about her.

"I'm sorry, Liam," she said.

"Don't be," he responded. "It's not your fault. Will you let me kiss you goodbye?"

Tears came into her eyes. "If you want to."

He turned her face to his, his fingers trembling against the curve of her cheek. "Sweetheart, you're more beautiful than ever, d'you know that?"

"But she's not for you, O'Grady!"

Miranda leapt to her feet. "Mind your own business, Adam Ferguson!" she shot back at him.

"You are my business," he said grimly. "And, as for you, O'Grady, you may be her manager at work, but that's as near as you'll get to her. If I catch you within five feet of her again, you'll take to your bed for another reason than the one you have in mind!"

"Adam!"

"Keep out of it, Miranda!"

"I will not! I'll not have you threatening Liam just because he's concerned about an old friend. If I choose to exchange a friendly kiss with Liam, it's got nothing to do with you!"

If she'd thought his eyes cold before, she could not make that complaint now. They were on fire with anger and they frightened her more than they ever had before.

"I'll deal with you later," he said coldly. "Suffice it to say, in Sri Lanka we do not kiss *anyone* in public! Not even *old friends!*"

"Oh, don't be so stuffy!" she retorted, abandoning all caution in one, wild throw at retrieving her independence.

She might have known it wouldn't work. He silenced her with a single, burning look, then turned his attention back to Liam O'Grady.

"She'll be back to work in the morning," he said briefly. "Under the circumstances it would be better if you didn't visit with us this afternoon. I'll accept this time that the woman tempted you—just so long as you keep your hands off her in the future!"

Miranda lifted her chin. "I may not want him to!"

"Your wishes are not being consulted," he bit out. "Keep out of this, Miranda, unless you want more trouble than you can handle!"

Liam O'Grady brushed his hands nervously together, not looking at either of the two protagonists. Miranda felt more abandoned than ever. First her mother and now Liam, both had failed her in their different ways. She would have thought that Liam would have had more spirit. Was he afraid of Adam, as she was?

"You'd better go, Liam," she said.

"Yes, I'd better!" the Irishman agreed. "Good luck, Miranda! I think you're going to need it!"

Miranda thought so too. She presented a cheek for his kiss. Liam backed away, glancing apprehensively at Adam as he did so.

"Perhaps you would prefer to shake hands!" Miranda said, annoyed.

Liam reddened then shook his head. "I'll see you in the morning," he mumbled. "God go with you, Miranda!"

Miranda sat down on the seat by the lake, crossing her legs to show him she was in no hurry to move away from her chosen spot. She ignored Adam, breathing deeply and evenly to give herself courage.

Adam sat down beside her, his face as stern and craggy as the surrounding mountains. "Miranda—"

"I don't wish to discuss it," she cut him off. "I shan't ever wish to discuss it with you. Liam is an old friend of mine—"

"Who wants to be your lover!"

"That's his business—and mine, not yours!"

Adam looked at her for a long moment in a brooding silence. Inwardly, Miranda quaked, but she gave no sign of it as she went on sitting there, motionless, looking out across the lake with unseeing eyes.

"What is that island used for?" she asked him when his silence had become unbearable to her.

He put out a hand, enfolding hers between warm fingers. "You have more courage than most women," he complimented her.

"I doubt it!" she retorted. "But I bow to your superior knowledge. You've known far more of the species than I have!"

"Very likely," he observed dryly, and she was surprised to see he was smiling at her in genuine amusement; "and more men too. It isn't kind to hold out hope to someone when there is none."

Miranda pulled on her hand, irritated. "When I want your advice, I'll ask for it!"

He threaded his fingers through hers, still smiling. "When I offer my advice, you'll take it, my dear."

Her anger was dying away and with it much of the

courage he had endowed her with. She felt all the more vulnerable as even while she hated him the touch of his hand against hers made her long to be closer still.

"What is that island?" she repeated.

"The kings of Kandy used it as a pleasure garden. They had a special barge that took them back and forth. It has long been thought that there's treasure at the bottom of the lake. Once some was found by a British Lieutenant when he was digging the foundations of a house near the lake. The then Governor, a man named Barnes, sent to England for a diving-bell, but it fell into a paddy-field on the last leg of its journey. It wouldn't have worked. The mud is fifteen feet deep in some places at the bottom, so he wouldn't have been able to see anything if he had gone down to look."

"I'd rather have the garden than the treasure," Miranda remarked.

"Then you're unique amongst women!" Adam assured her. Then he asked, "Are you ready for lunch now?"

"I'd rather go back to the hotel," she said. "I've held up the others for long enough."

His fingers tightened on hers until she expected her bones to give way beneath the pressure. "I meant what I said about O'Grady!"

"You're hurting me!" she complained.

"I'll do more than hurt you if I catch you encouraging any other man to have what is mine!" he said, but he relaxed his hold, examining her reddened fingers with a rueful look. "Lunch will do us both good," he went on more lightly. "The sooner we're married the better! You won't be thinking of O'Grady then!"

Miranda felt a sharp shaft of desire fan out from deep within her. It seemed superfluous for her to mention that she wasn't thinking of Liam O'Grady now or then. It was Adam Ferguson who filled her mind and her heart, and the knowledge that she would never be more than a convenience to him in his bed and in his home gave her thoughts of him a bitter-sweet flavour that would not go away.

"You make too much of too little," she told him.

His eye-lids flickered uncharacteristically, almost as if he had been on the point of saying something else.

"As long as it stays that way," he said.

Chapter Eight

Miranda enjoyed herself that afternoon. She had thought she wouldn't. She had thought that her worries about the future and her concern for Liam's feelings would have prevented it, but partly because everything was new to her and partly because Adam was with her, she had a very good time.

Adam took her to friends for lunch, a young couple engaged in the restoration of some of Ceylon's ancient and once lost cities and who had a passion for their island's history that was very engaging.

"Have you been to Polonnaruwa or Anuradhapura yet?" the wife had asked Miranda.

"I can't even pronounce them!" Miranda had replied.

"You will learn. Adam is bound to take you to see them sooner or later."

Miranda had been surprised that he should be interested in such things. "His tea estate is too important to him to have much interest in anything else," she had hazarded.

"Where did you get that idea? He has often helped us, working as a coolie in the hot sun, carrying stones and cement up and down countless steps, when we have been restoring one of the stupas!"

Miranda had been obliged to confess her ignorance. "What is a stupa?"

The young wife had laughed. "I suppose you might call it a pagoda, though that summons up to the mind a Chinese or Japanese structure, such as you have in Kew Gardens. They are those bell-like shapes you see in Buddist temples everywhere. Often they have a relic buried in their foundations, but sometimes they don't. They serve to recall the purpose of life to the mind."

Miranda had been fascinated. "Have you been to Kew?" she had asked curiously.

"You bet! Have you been to our Botanical Gardens?"

Miranda had shaken her head. "I want to see it more than anything. I've been trying to persuade the people I'm working with to use them as a backdrop for a part of the collection we're photographing, but I haven't had any success so far!"

On hearing how little of Ceylon Miranda had seen, her hostess turned imperiously to the men. "Adam, how is it Miranda has seen nothing of our country yet?"

"She's always working," he complained.

"Well, she is not working this afternoon. We are going to the Botanical Gardens—"

Adam favoured her with a slanting smile. "*We* are going to the Gardens," he corrected her.

Her eyes laughed at him. "How do you know you won't find Nihal and I there before you?"

Adam showed no sign of resenting her teasing. "What a very romantic notion for two people who had never met before they married!" he had drawled, his grey eyes on Miranda's shocked face. "Miranda tries not to believe in the power of her destiny. I expect you to persuade her otherwise."

Anula had laughed out loud. "She doesn't have to believe! Hasn't Sita told her whether a match with you will be auspicious or not?"

"But surely," Miranda had protested, "you don't believe in that sort of thing?"

"But it's true!" Anula had assured her. "Nihal's chart and mine fit together exactly and there is never a cross word between us!"

"There are plenty of cross words between us!" Miranda had replied dryly.

But Anula had dismissed that as being of little moment. "It is hard when one is not yet married," she had said wisely. "I was as nervous as—what is your expression—as a cat on a hot tin roof, as my parents will tell you! It would have been worse if I had known Nihal before we could be together." She had jumped to her feet. "Come, we shall have lunch!"

Lunch had been a lazy meal of curry and rice, followed by fruit and the tea Adam had promised her, spiced with ginger and sweetened with a palm candy called jaggery. It wasn't much like the tea Miranda had always drunk in England. This was a clear, golden drink, served in a glass, and which was refreshing and cooling at the same time, much like the curry had been before it. "If you eat rice and curry at midday, you will never suffer from the bad tummy some of the European tourists get when they come here," Anula had instructed Miranda solemnly. "It matters less at night, but in the heat of the day it is essential to eat as we eat. Remember that when you are married and have the ordering of Adam's house!"

"If I ever do," Miranda had retorted.

Anula had stared at her, her eyes wide. "Is *she* still there? I thought, as Adam spoke only of you, she might have gone?"

Miranda had silently shaken her head. The other girl's sympathy was unwelcome to her, confirming her fears that Anne Forster was a real danger to her and that the whole thing was not something in her imagination.

Anula had looked hastily away. "Perhaps he doesn't feel the same as he did about her. She has never been well-liked amongst us, but of course it's a different matter amongst her own people. Adam has always been one of us," Anula said, "but his step-mother and brother were always unhappy amongst us. Mrs. Forster is like them."

The Ceylonese girl said nothing more, plainly embarrassed by the whole situation. Miranda did not press her. It was only what she had already known, after all. Adam and Anne had once been lovers and they probably would be again. As Adam's wife, she would be expected to stand on the sidelines and do nothing to prevent it. Adam had practically told her as much!

They went to watch the dancers after lunch. Miranda had seen them in the procession, but that had given her no idea of the intricacy of their movements and the beautiful control they had over the least gesture, each one having a different meaning.

"Had enough?" Adam asked her quietly.

She had known he was standing behind her. She had felt the heat of his body and the tensing of her own muscles in response to his closeness. He had not had to touch her for her senses to leap and for her heart to race, distracting her from the spectacle of the dance no matter how hard she tried to concentrate on its magnificent detail.

"If Anula wants to come to the Gardens—"

"Her husband can take her."

"But I—"

His grey eyes mocked her. "You don't want to be alone with me?"

The colour burned her throat and face. "They are such a nice couple!" she defended herself.

"Aren't they? But I'd rather have you to myself this afternoon. You'll be safe enough amongst the orchids, which I couldn't promise you if I were to take you home. I'll fetch the Landrover."

His dry tones brought a fever to her blood. She would not be safe with him anywhere, but not because of him, but because of herself! She hoped that he didn't know that, but the slight smile on his lips told her how idle such a hope was. Of course he knew! He knew entirely too much about her. Sometimes she thought that he could read her mind. It was positively uncanny!

While he was gone she tried to cool her emotions. She had never danced like a puppet on a string for any man before, so why should she now? But when she saw him returning her breath caught in the back of her throat and every nerve quivered in anticipation! Involuntarily her glance rested on his firmly chiselled mouth and she could feel again its pressure on hers. She tossed her head to dismiss the fancy, but her lips tingled with desire for his kiss and she turned her head away so he could not read her eyes.

She stood a little to one side while he thanked his friends for lunch and answered their questions about his marriage.

"My place has been neglected long enough," he explained. "I want my children to know the estate as I knew it before my mother died."

"Has Lionel nothing to say to that?" they asked him.

"His sons will be born in England, mine will follow me here!"

Anula's liquid dark eyes slid from his face to Miranda's. "Your wife-to-be is an Englishwoman," she reminded him.

Adam's hand descended on Miranda's shoulder. "There are English women and English women. Miranda will live where I live!"

A worried frown came and went between Anula's fine eyes. "Everybody frets for their own sometimes, Adam. Even I long for Colombo sometimes, and when I do, I go for a visit to my family and all is well again."

"England is a long, long way away," Miranda said faintly.

"Not too far for a visit!" Anula claimed.

"It'll be better, at first, for Miranda's mother to visit us here," Adam decided firmly. "It'll be a year or two before I can get away for any length of time."

Nihal looked at him sharply. "How's it going?" he asked, successfully diverted.

A glow of excitement crossed Adam's face. "I'm nearly there! All will be well just as long as I can keep Anne under my eye. Fortunately, at the moment, she has no desire to be anywhere else!"

"And Miranda's presence doesn't complicate things too much?"

"Not so far." Adam's eyes glinted dangerously as Miranda made a movement of protest. "Miranda's not my keeper, nor will she be after we're married. Both she and Anne know that."

Anula's lower lip was caught between her teeth and her expression was one of sympathy for the English girl. "Anne has no scruples—" she began to say.

"Nor have I!" Adam cut her off.

"Then see that Miranda doesn't suffer," Anula said gently. "Between you, you may hurt her."

"That's my affair," Adam said pleasantly, but he was not to be gainsaid and Miranda felt a shiver go down her spine.

"Isn't it mine too?" she asked as casually as she could.

His eyes narrowed and she found it impossible to guess what he was thinking, then he said, "Your part is to trust me, Miranda, and keep your nose out of my business. You'll be happier if you do!"

He could not have made it clearer that she was to have no real part in his life. Obviously, his sister-in-law meant more to him than she did. If physical satisfaction was all he wanted from Miranda why had he not taken her when she had offered herself? Were children so important to him that he couldn't wait for the woman he loved to become their mother?

The Royal Botanical Gardens were about four miles outside Kandy on the Colombo road. Miranda sat beside Adam in the Landrover and tried to pretend to herself she was a normal, ecstatic engaged girl setting out to spend the afternoon with her fiancé, but she was not very successful. One glance at Adam's stony face was enough to remind her that there was no love in his regard for her. He looked more angry than loving, though whether he was angry with her or with himself she had no means of knowing.

"Are you interested in plants and growing things?" she asked him.

"Most creepers are," he said.

"Creepers?"

"An apprentice tea planter."

"But you're not an apprentice, surely?"

"I was once." He sighed. "My father insisted, though there was little chance of my actually growing the stuff. My stepmother wouldn't have me at home, so I went and worked for Nihal's father. I came back after Lionel inherited the estate to manage the place for him. I wanted to live in my own house."

With Anne? But why ask the question? It was obvious that Anne had married the richer brother, but she had been in love with the poorer, and he with her.

Adam bought the tickets at the entrance while Miranda admired a striking row of Queen of Flowering Trees just inside the park. Further on there were walks edged with many coloured bougainvillaeas, ranging from the distinctive purple to salmon pink, reds, and violets.

"How my mother would love it here!" Miranda sighed. "She is quite a gardener herself, but we don't have anything like this in England!"

"No? I thought English gardens were famous throughout the world."

"They are, especially our cottage gardens. We have the best lawns in the world and gorgeous roses, but I've never seen color like this before. It dazzles the eyes!"

Adam shot her a sidewise glance. "Wait until you see our orchids."

She made a face at him. "I don't much care for orchids. I don't like green flowers, no matter how rare—"

"Wait and see!" he cut her off.

But it was a long time before they went into the glass houses that held the orchids and the other, more exotic, species of flowers. Miranda was more than content to wander around the park and have Adam tell her about the different trees she could see there. She was astonished at the many varieties of flowering trees, all of them generous in their blooms and striking to the eye. There were Flame trees from Madagascar, the Queen of Flowering trees she had already seen, with their pink and yellow flowers, from Burma and Malacca, Jacaranda trees, mauve and cool, and the Giant Bamboo of Burma, the largest known bamboo that grows anything from ninety to a hundred-and-thirty feet high, with stems of ten inches in diameter. These last grow so rapidly they can achieve their full height in two or three months.

There was a magnificent specimen of the Cajeput-oil tree of Moluccas, and behind it the famous "Upas" tree of Java, sometimes called the Ordeal-poison tree, as at one time it was supposed to exude poisonous fumes fatal to man and beast alike. The sap of the bark contains a deadly poison called "Ipoh" which was, and probably still is, used for poisoning the tips of arrows and darts. Only a little further on was the Sack Tree of Sri Lanka with its similar use to mankind.

In contrast was the Madara, whose function was the exact opposite, it having been said that anyone carrying a piece of its wood was protected against wild animals and snakes. Miranda wondered if its properties would protect her against human animals also and, if she had not thought it too superstitious to contemplate, she would have armed herself with a tiny piece to ward off Anne's powers. As it was, she crumbled a tiny piece of its bark between her fingers, her blue-black hair falling forward to hide her face as she did so.

"Will you be finished with your assignment in three days?" Adam asked her suddenly.

She pushed her hair back over her shoulders. "Maybe."

"I want to be married on Saturday."

"Saturday?" It was less than a week to Saturday. Her fingers trembled and caught in her hair as she contemplated the trap he was setting for her. "Why do we have to be in such a hurry?"

"You know why."

She was startled into looking at him. "I don't know why you want to marry me," she was goaded into saying.

"I want you, Miranda. What's more, you want me."

"That's not the only reason for marriage," she said.

His face could have been chiselled out of stone for all the emotion it displayed. "You'll be happier married," he told her.

She bit her lip. "Will you be happier too?"

He was silent for a long moment. "I told you, I want children. A man has to have a wife for that."

"Otherwise you wouldn't bother?" she pressed him.

"I might not. Does it matter, Miranda?"

"It matters to me!"

His lips twisted into a wry smile. *"Marriage* matters to you! I'm offering you marriage. What more do you want?"

"You may call it marriage, I don't! A wife has a place in a man's life and in his—in his heart! You don't care about me at all!"

He caught her arm, caressing the inside of her wrist with his forefinger. "I could make you promises I can't keep," he said abruptly. "Instead, I'm being honest with you, or as honest as I can be." His fingers tightened about her wrist. "Can you be ready by Saturday?"

It took all her courage to answer him. "Don't you have any feelings for anyone at all?" she asked him.

His mouth tightened. "Only a woman would want her heart to rule her head! It doesn't last, Miranda. My father was besotted by his second wife, but he hated her in the end!"

"And so you won't allow yourself to love anyone?"

He shrugged his shoulders. "I could answer that better if I knew what love is. I know I want you and that's enough for me. The loving, if there is any, will have to be on your side!"

The park receded from her vision. She saw only his cold grey eyes willing her to surrender herself into his keeping. It was madness, she knew, but she could not imagine life without him. She might be unhappy with him often, but there would be moments of supreme happiness too. If she concentrated on them perhaps the rest would be bearable. It would have to be, because she couldn't say no to him . . . ever . . .

"Starting on Saturday?" she said with a choking laugh.

"You won't regret it," he assured her.

"I hope not." Her eyes pricked with tears. "I hope neither of us will regret it."

His hands spread across her back, arousing a shiver that brought a gleam of male triumph to his eyes. "It's long enough to wait for you! I ache with my need to have you in my bed and to awaken with you in my arms!"

As he had done with how many women before her? Certainly with Anne! And what if he was disappointed in his brand new wife? Miranda felt a churning in her innards as she measured her own lack of experience against his undoubted expertise.

Her lashes fluttered nervously and she pulled away from him. "On Saturday then," she confirmed breathlessly. "I hope you're not expecting too much—"

To her indignation he threw back his head and laughed. "You don't have to worry, Miranda," he said, pulling gently on a lock of her blue-black hair, "I'll take what I want and you'll soon come to like it that way. I shan't expect more of you than you have to give."

She was shocked by his frankness. "How do you know?" she asked curiously.

He laughed again. "I know a great deal about you! More than you probably know yourself, my dear little innocent!"

"I'll have to ask Liam and the girls to come to our wedding," she put in quickly, embarrassed. "He will want to come anyway."

Adam shrugged massive shoulders. "Poor fool! I wouldn't go to see you married to another man, knowing that all that sweetness belonged to him and could never be mine. I'd try to forget you as soon as I could!"

"And would you succeed?" Miranda asked, her voice dropping to a whisper.

A shadow passed over his face. "Why not?" he said indifferently.

The orchids amazed Miranda with their beauty. There were hardly any green ones at all. They came in all the colours of the rainbow and, for the first time in her life, she understood how they had come to exercise such a fascination for so many people. Their delicate blooms were perfect, without any fading that more ordinary flowers are subject to. There was only one among their number that Miranda disliked. It was one she had seen before and on which she had based her claim to dislike the whole specie. It was a yellowy-green, with unhealthy brown spots and, as soon as her eye fell on it, she knew why she had never cared for its exotic splendour. It reminded her of Anne Forster. Indeed, it was almost the same colour as the other girl's fair hair in certain lights, and Anne too, had brown spots on her skin. Miranda had noticed them on her hands.

To reach the Orchid House they had to pass under an archway covered in the creeper Cinderella Slipper which Miranda liked almost as well as the orchids. She wondered aloud which was Adam's favourite and he pointed it out to her with a sudden softening of his expression.

"It's called the Vesak Orchid and it's endemic to

Sri Lanka. Perhaps that's why I like it," he told her. "It comes in a violet pink that would look good on you with your black hair, and sometimes, though rarely, it's as white as your fair skin. Altogether it reminds me of you!"

Was he teasing? Miranda couldn't tell. Though his tone was gentle, almost affectionate, his expression was enigmatic. She put a light hand on his arm. "Adam, I'm getting a little tired. Will you take me back to the hotel? If I'm to be ready by Saturday I'll have to work all the hours there are until then."

"Good, as long as you're too busy to play around with O'Grady."

"Liam is a friend," she protested.

"That doesn't change how he feels about you, my sweet."

"No, but it changes everything else. Liam wouldn't dream of playing around, as you so elegantly put it, with another man's fiancée. He's not like that!"

"Every man is like that," Adam contradicted her flatly. "Keep out of his way is my advice to you—it's the kindest thing you can do for him!"

Miranda had already come to that conclusion for herself, but she wasn't going to make any promises to Adam about how she was going to treat someone she had known far longer than she had known him.

"Shall we go?" she suggested steadily.

Outside again in the fresh air, Miranda paused to look at the water plants, the most imposing of which was the Giant Water Lily, called in Latin after Queen Victoria but sharing little else with that tiny and forthright monarch. Miranda was more pleased with the lotus, the red and white which are offered in the temples, and the other blue and white ones which for some reason are not.

"I thought you'd be here, Adam," Anne's voice interrupted her thoughts. "I've come to relieve your boredom by asking you to take me back to the bungalow with you."

"Delighted," said Adam.

Miranda turned to say hullo and almost took a step backwards into the water when she saw the venom in Anne's blue eyes. "Are we to have the pleasure of your company tonight?" the older girl drawled out of the side of her mouth.

"No, I shall be working," Miranda replied.

Anne wound Adam's arm about her body, looking up at him with a soft, feminine, affectionate look that aroused a new and painful emotion in Miranda that she had never known before. *She was jealous,* and, judging by the look on Adam's face, she had cause to be.

"Then we shall have the evening to ourselves," Anne went on in the same smooth tone. A faint smile curved her too thin lips. "It will be quite like old times, won't it?" she added. "Before Miranda; before Lionel; before any of them came into our paradise to disturb us. . . ."

Chapter Nine

By Friday night Miranda and the whole team were completely exhausted.

"So he's talked you into an early wedding?" Liam O'Grady had said wryly to Miranda. "Wouldn't it be better to be certain you're going to be happy with him first?"

"How can I be certain?" Miranda had retorted unanswerably.

"You could at least be sure that you want to marry him!"

"I am!" Miranda had claimed. She did want to marry Adam Ferguson, the Adam Ferguson she imagined she could glimpse at intervals behind the hard, cynical man whose dislike of women was as strong as his determination to wed her as quickly as possible.

"Okay, okay," Liam retired, defeated, "so you want to marry him! You're scared stiff of him, and you don't like the setup, but you're going to marry him. The trouble with you, my girl, is that you're not using your head!"

Miranda eased aching shoulders. "You could be right," she had acknowledged. "But the alternative doesn't look so hot either."

Liam's lips had twisted into the mockery of a smile. "That puts me in my place! Don't blame me when things go wrong for you! I'll be waiting in the wings for you to come to your senses, as you must do sooner or later."

"And what if I don't?" Miranda had asked him. "You'd do much better to put me out of your mind, Liam. I'd be a different person anyway to the one you thought you knew."

"Are you?" asked Liam. "I wonder."

Lying on her bed in the hotel, trying to raise the energy to change and go and join the others for dinner, she had thought again about the patient, stubborn expression Liam displayed whenever he had come near her. Try as she would, her sympathy had changed to impatience, and she had found herself avoiding him as often as she could, preferring the garrulous company of the two girls if she could not get away by herself, using the excuse that she had to develop her films and plan the next session's work.

She had seen nothing of Adam for days, yet he was always there at the back of her mind, especially in this room. She half expected to see him standing in her room, waiting for her, and every time it came as a disappointment that he wasn't there.

The telephone shrilled beside her, making her

jump. She reached out for the receiver, her heart thumping, as she thought it might be Adam.

"Thinking of me?" he asked her.

She would have denied it if she could, but she was too honest to dissemble easily, and the sound of his voice had scattered her wits, leaving her defenceless and dry of mouth.

"I was, as a matter of fact," she admitted. "Liam—"

"Forget him!"

"You ask too much!" she told him tartly. "You have from the very beginning!"

"You wouldn't be so provocative if I was there beside you, my lovely Miranda. There would be no room for O'Grady in your thoughts then! Have you finished your assignment?"

"Yes, I have—just. I hadn't realised how much we still had to do. The girls have been wonderful!"

"But not O'Grady?"

"Him too," Miranda admitted. She didn't care for the dry note in Adam's voice. Was it possible that he knew how quickly she had tired of Liam's wounded face? She found she had a weapon of her own in hand, not realising it was a boomerang as she threw it at him.

"How is Anne?"

"Delectable." He sounded as smug as a cat with a saucer of cream.

"And Lionel?"

"Out of sight is out of mind."

Could he be speaking of herself? Miranda thought miserably. She hadn't had sight or sound of Adam for three whole days and Anne had been in the same house with him. Jealousy made her throat ache and her tongue feel like a lump of wood in her mouth.

"That might work two ways," she reminded Adam. "Perhaps he's forgotten all about her. Perhaps," she added more dangerously, "I forgot all about you while I was working with Liam!"

"Did you?" The arrogant question expected only one answer, but she wasn't going to give him the satisfaction of uttering it.

"Out of sight is out of mind," she quoted his own answer.

"We both know whom you belong to, Miranda, even if you don't want to admit it."

She gulped. "You can't know that!"

His laughter mocked her. "Can't I? Think back, Miranda, and then deny that it's my image which is imprinted on your heart and mind. Tomorrow—"

"You take too much for granted!" she scolded. "I may have changed my mind about tomorrow. I may not want to marry you!"

"You'll be here, if I have to drag you here by your luscious black hair! That's what I'm calling about. Anne has offered to fetch you out here tomorrow morning—"

"I'd rather come on my own!"

"And I'd rather you didn't come with O'Grady! Anne will pick you up at the hotel at ten o'clock. Have you got something suitable to wear?"

Miranda reviewed her wardrobe with a sinking heart. "What is suitable? I haven't got a wedding dress tucked away, if that's what you mean."

"Have you something else you want to wear?"

She cursed herself that she hadn't given a thought to all this before. "I haven't much with me, not of the formal variety of dress. I have a three-quarter length—"

"If it fits you, you can wear my mother's dress," Adam interrupted her.

"Your *mother's?*"

"*My* mother's. Have you any objection to wearing a second-hand dress?"

Now that was more like him! Not a sentimental keepsake after all, only a second-hand dress! Her eyes stung with tears and her voice shook.

"I think I might like to wear something of your mother's." She didn't add that his mother had been the only woman she had ever heard him refer to in terms of any liking or respect.

"I thought you might," was all he said.

"Yes, but, Adam, what if it doesn't fit me?"

"Sita can alter it for you." There was a pause. "Sita works for me now. Anne sacked her yesterday, told her to get out and go back to her family. They're very poor though and they can't afford another mouth to feed. I told her she can stay on as your personal maid."

"I've never had a maid in my life!"

"She'll find something to do for you." There was a pent-up anger in his voice that told her this was not the moment to argue the point with him. "She used to work for my stepmother in the house. One of these days I'll show you the 'lines' where most of our Tamil workers live. Then you'll see why I can't allow her to be sent back there."

"But why did Anne fire her?"

She could almost hear Adam shrugging his shoulders. "One of those explosive bouts of bad temper women are prone to—"

"Not all women!"

"No? You sounded as though you were getting ready to give me the rough side of your tongue when I first called.'"

Had she? If she had, she wasn't going to admit it. "If I sounded anything it was exhausted," she said firmly. "Have you any idea how hard we've all been working these last few days to keep your deadline?"

"It kept you from getting into trouble with O'Grady," Adam said in tones intended to nettle her. "Get a good night's sleep tonight because I can't guarantee you the same tomorrow! I'll see you in the morning?"

She wondered if she should remind him it was unlucky for the bridegroom to see his bride before the ceremony. She had the feeling he wouldn't have much sympathy with such nonsense—and yet he had encouraged Sita to spell out her destiny from her birth chart. Had that only been because he had already been thinking she would be a suitable brood-mare to bear his children?

"I'll be there. Goodnight, Adam."

He lowered his voice until she could hardly hear him, and she was sure it was the distortion of the telephone system that made him sound so unexpectedly tender.

"Sweet dreams, Miranda!"

She lay back against the pillows, trying to still the

eager clamour of her senses that wanted more of Adam than just the sound of his voice. That, at least, would be solved by their marriage tomorrow, she thought, but none of the other problems were likely to be. What did Anne think of Adam's taking a wife? Did she think Miranda of such little account that she could safely ignore her? Would Adam continue his affair with her? Miranda had no means of knowing, but she doubted he would have any greater respect for his marriage vows than Anne had had for hers.

She drifted off to sleep and in her dreams, Adam spoke to her in the gentle, tender tones he had used on the telephone, and he was as much in love with her as she was with him.

Anne came at exactly ten o'clock. She didn't get out of the car, but put her palm down on the horn and yelled out of the window at the hall porter.

"Fetch Miss Wade!"

Miranda came out of the front door and climbed into the passenger seat beside her. It was a German car, new and shiny, and with every gadget one could possibly want laid out before the driver.

"Is that all the luggage you have?" Anne enquired, frowning over her shoulder as the porter stowed Miranda's single case in the boot at the back.

"There are my cameras. I told them to put them in on top. One can't bring much on an aeroplane."

"Ah yes, your cameras! I expected you to go about as some tourists do, with cameras slung from every limb! Don't you carry one at all?"

Miranda produced the miniature camera she usually carried in the pocket of her jacket. "I have this one. I prefer one of the bigger ones for serious studies, but this takes excellent snaps, and often they turn out to be the best of all."

The lid of the boot slammed shut and the porter brought the keys back to Anne, who flung them into her bag with a sour look.

"Adam says it's why you want to stay on out here. You're going to do a book of photographs? Couldn't you do that without marrying Adam?"

"Yes, I could."

"Then why marry him?"

Miranda went cold inside. "Is that any business of yours?"

The car shot forward, causing Anne to slam on the brakes as they approached the main road. She drove, Miranda thought, as she did everything else, according to her mood, and she was not in a good mood this morning.

"That's why I volunteered to fetch you this morning," Anne Forster said, flashing a smile. "There's a great deal you don't know about Adam. His business is my business, and it always will be, married or not. He knows why I married Lionel, but it didn't make any difference to *us*. Your marriage won't either."

"Isn't that up to Adam and me?"

"My dear girl, don't be naïve! Adam doesn't like or trust any woman—he never has! But he uses us, and he knows I'm not above using him! He even admires me for it. He can't stand being fussed over

and made much of—that's the mistake you've made!
He knows you're head over heels in love with him,
but it won't make him any kinder towards you.
You're a fool if you think it will! He sees you as a
tool in his war against me, but you won't last! Adam
is mine, and Adam must be brought to understand
that little fact. I can always switch back to Lionel if
Adam doesn't cooperate. Then he won't have
anything, neither me, or the tea estate. It will all be
Lionel's—and mine!"

Miranda studied her hands, feeling slightly sick.
"What does Lionel—"

"Lionel does as he's told!"

"As I shall have to?" Miranda said, bitterly.

"Adam wants a child and I can't have one. You
won't last longer than that," Anne assured her
grimly. "Your presence is strictly temporary and
doesn't bother me too much. But, fair's fair, I've
thought all along that you ought to be told where
you stand. At least I did that much for Lionel! He
always knew I'd leave him for Adam if Adam could
get his tea estate back from him. I'm not the sort of
person who lives on fresh air!"

Judging by the car she drove that was an understatement. Miranda tried to make her mind a blank,
but she couldn't shut out the wave of pain. So that
was the reason why Adam was marrying her: *Anne
couldn't have children,* and Adam wanted a son to
come after him. It was as simple as that.

Anne turned her head and looked at her passenger, her blue eyes as hard as the sapphire rings on
her hands.

"Shall I take you back to the hotel?"

Miranda shook her head. She found herself thinking of what Anula had said, that she had met Adam on an auspicious day and that he was a lucky man. If she couldn't quite believe in such things herself, many, many people did. She was not thinking of the people who looked up their stars in the daily paper back in England and as promptly forgot what they said the day would hold for them; she was thinking of the serious believers, statesmen and others, all over Asia, whose whole lives were ruled by their birth-charts and thus by the stars. She was thinking of Sita.

"If my marriage is going to be such a short one, I'd better make the most of it!" she said. "I told Adam I'd be there."

"He can find someone else to mother his child!"

"He's already found me."

"I'd thought better of you," Anne said coldly. "Haven't you any pride at all? You may think yourself to be in love with him, but you don't have to ruin your whole future for a few nights in his arms! That's what I'm trying to tell you, Miranda! I'll get you out of all this, if you'll let me!"

Miranda threaded her fingers together to stop them from trembling. She would probably be hurt, just as Anne was warning her she would be, but she was going to marry Adam all the same. She had to marry him. It wasn't only that she wanted him so badly that her body ached with its need for him; it was to do with his mother's wedding dress, and the note in his voice when he had wished her sweet dreams the night before, and the sharp way he had spoken of Liam O'Grady, almost as if he had been jealous of him.

"Adam has my promise," she said aloud, "and I keep my promises."

"More fool you! Nobody will expect you to keep your marriage vows, however. Adam certainly won't!"

"That's up to Adam."

Anne's gaze was scornful. "You don't really mean to be faithful and true for as long as you live, do you?"

Miranda licked dry lips. "I think so," she said.

"Have you told Adam that?"

Was it possible that Anne was less sure of herself than she was pretending? Miranda felt a moment of hope that was instantly quelled as she remembered how Adam had welcomed her arrival in the Botanical Gardens.

"He hasn't asked me. He's told me quite a few things about what he expects from marriage, but he hasn't asked me what I expect. He may be surprised when he does!"

The car almost ran off the road into the ditch. Anne wrenched at the wheel, her fingers showing white, so intense was her grasp.

"What do you mean?" she rasped out.

Miranda lifted her head high. "I mean that not even Adam can make me renege on the kind of person I know myself to be. I love him very much—you're right about that!—I love him far more than my own happiness, or even my own comfort. I think he'll come to understand that in the end. Adam thinks of women as being you and his stepmother, but his mother was a woman too. I think she was a better model than either of you."

Looking at Anne's stricken face, Miranda felt much better. She smiled sweetly. "Shall I drive the rest of the way?" she offered blandly. She was still smiling when they drove up outside Adam's bungalow.

Chapter Ten

Sita oversaw Miranda's toilette with a ruthless efficiency that secretly amused her new mistress.

"Stand still, Miss Miranda! How d'you expect me to fix these skirts if you will wander about the room that way? We'll never have you ready at this rate!"

Miranda gave up trying to sneak a view of herself in the glass and resigned herself to being pushed and pulled about for a little while longer. Adam's mother's wedding dress was everything she had hoped it would be. It was fashioned of hand-made lace, lace made on the island Sita had told her, and worn over a shift of red silk, because scarlet was the colour chosen by most Ceylonese for their wedding dresses, particularly the Hindus.

Indeed, Miranda began to wonder if she were going to have a Christian ceremony at all. The Estate Tamils were all *en fete* for the day and she had already been greeted by the small, wiry man who was the priest in charge of the small temple used by the Hindu workers. He had met her with garlands of flowers and many prayers chanted through his broken teeth.

Miranda had thanked him, as solemn as he, but Anne had swept past them both, still in a rage at someone else being in the centre of the stage.

Sita had pulled at her arm. "You must visit the temple later," she had bidden her, "but now you must come and get ready!"

"Time for your shower, Miss Miranda!" The dress was eased off her shoulders and fell to her feet. "Don't forget to scent the water! A bride must go to her husband smelling as sweet as the flowers!" Sita surveyed Miranda's small collection of beauty aids in dismay. "Are these all you have? Have you no special scent you wish to wear today?"

"I thought—"

Sita looked positively distraught. "I could fetch you one of Miss Anne's perfumes, but it would not go well with you—"

"And she might find out!" Miranda reminded her, suppressing a grin.

"I will find you *something!* Will you please hurry, Miss Miranda!"

Miranda obediently hurried through her shower, thinking how strange it was to have a personal maid to prepare her for her wedding. She had always imagined she would be married in the parish church of Winchelsea and that it would be her mother who would have helped her get ready for the great occasion. Winchelsea and her mother seemed very far away. Too far for her comfort. She had few allies to make her feel at home here, a stranger in a strange land.

Sita returned with half-a-dozen little bottles which she put on the dressing-table. "They come from the women of my family," she announced, her eyes flashing in case Miranda should take it into her head to argue with her. "Whoever heard of a bride going to the marriage-bed unperfumed? And you have too few clothes! You must buy more when you are a married woman."

"Perhaps I will," Miranda consoled her.

Sita nodded eagerly. "Many, many pretty things!" She picked up Miranda's nightdress with a gesture of distaste. "You should have told me before and I would have seen you had something more fitting!"

"But I like—"

Sita shook her head sadly. "On your wedding night you should have something as light and as pretty as a butterfly's wings."

Miranda gave up the unequal battle and abandoned herself to Sita's ministrations as though she had no mind or will of her own. It was better not to think too much, she told herself.

When she was dressed and ready, she felt more as if she were a candidate for some oriental harem than an ordinary English girl going to her wedding.

"May I look at myself now?" she asked Sita.

Sita led her to the full-length glass. "The dress was made for someone with the same colouring," she whispered to her. "Mr. Ferguson's mother had dark hair also."

"And the second Mrs. Ferguson?"

Sita's face went blank. "She was fair, Miss Miranda. She had yellow hair, not pale like Miss Anne's, but the colour of this jug." She pointed to a brass jug filled with perfumed water.

"Did you know Adam's mother?" Miranda asked her.

Sita nodded. "For a short time only. Mr. Ferguson brought me up to the house to serve her when my own mother died. There was talk of my going to India, but I've never been there."

"Was your mother all the family you had here?"

"She was a picker. My father is an old man now, supported by my sisters. He has never earned much money."

Miranda turned impulsively. "Sita, what was it that you and Mrs. Forster quarrelled about?"

Sita was cautious. "Why do you want to know? Why don't you ask Miss Anne?"

"Because she wouldn't tell me the truth," Miranda said frankly.

"No," Sita agreed. "She doesn't like your being here. She likes to think of this house as hers."

"Perhaps she has reason to. Adam doesn't show any sign of asking her to go, does he?"

"Your husband plays his own game."

Miranda sighed. "I like the look of Anne's hand better than my own," she said more to herself than to the maid.

"Then you are foolish! Only the greedy want everything at once, the rest of us have to be content with a small piece of happiness at a time! When Mr. Ferguson is ready, he will make his own decisions."

"Anne is his brother's wife!"

Sita laughed, putting a nervous hand over her mouth as she did so. Her knowing eyes appraised Miranda's innocence. "That one is no husband to her, nor she a wife to him!"

"Is that why she came here?"

But Sita refused to answer. "It's time to go, Miss Miranda. You are looking very beautiful!"

Miranda's eyes caught and held Sita's face in the glass. "I have to know, Sita, has she any real claim on him?"

Sita's lip curled with a contempt that she seldom allowed her European employers to see. "Miss Anne is not a woman at all. There are bodies that go about the world looking like real people, but they have no souls to animate them, no spirit to live on after them. They are material things and have never learned wisdom." Sita paused.

Miranda would have pressed her further, but she felt that Sita had said all that she wanted to. She knew that it would be useless to ask Sita why she and Anne had quarreled. Sita had already answered the question obliquely and with dignity.

However, it was clear that she didn't like Anne any better than Miranda did. Had Anne treated the maid as one of her possessions? Miranda thought it quite likely, but she would have thought Sita would have been accustomed to such treatment. It couldn't have been the first time that Anne had spoken to her as though she was not a person at all, but an animated convenience to herself.

Miranda was going to ask Sita if they had quarrelled over her, but she knew the Tamil girl wouldn't tell her if they had. She changed her mind so abruptly that the sounds of speech were already beginning to come out of her mouth.

"Will Adam find me beautiful?" she asked instead.

"He will find in you a part of himself," said Sita.

Adam's rib! "And what will I find?" Miranda couldn't resist asking.

Sita trembled with shy laughter. "Your destiny, Miss Miranda. That was seen from the first time you came here, no?"

The Estate-workers were enjoying their holiday. They lined up outside the bungalow, their hands full of small gifts: flowers, fruits, and some of the spices which had first attracted the Europeans to this beautiful island. Miranda would have enjoyed herself too, if she could have brought herself to believe that she was actually married to the man who walked by her side. She had not seen him dressed in a Western-style suit before, complete with collar and tie and, whilst she thought he looked very well in it, she much preferred him as she had first seen him, naked to the waist and with only a sarong around his hips.

"Aren't these flowers beautiful!" Miranda exclaimed, accepting yet more perfect blossoms from a group of children. "And what are these?"

"Cinnamon," Adam told her. "It comes from a glossy evergreen bush which is a native of Sri Lanka. The spice is in the bark, peeled off, dried, and looking like that."

"I thought it was a powder," Miranda said.

He cast his eyes heavenwards. "Such straits have modern cooks come to! Cinnamon, my dear, is probably the oldest spice known to man, and one of my favourites. I hope you will know how to use it when you cook for me?" His eyes were mocking.

"I'm a very ordinary cook," she said nervously, "but I suppose I could learn to make the dishes you like."

"From Anne?"

She winced. "I should think Sita would make a better tutor."

"Perhaps. With Anne in her present mood we're more likely to be poisoned than wined and dined in style."

Miranda listened to his wry tones with a sinking heart. "Do you mind?" she hazarded, not daring to look at him.

"I daresay you will suffer more from her tongue than I. Bear with her, Miranda. She can't understand why I married you in such a hurry and may make us all uncomfortable for a while."

Miranda's eyes blurred. "You should have thought of that before!"

He slanted a smile at her. "You will make it up to me! In that dress, you look more than worth all the trouble you're going to bring me!"

Miranda tightened her hold on the flowers she was holding, bruising them with the pressure of her fingers. "I think it would be better if you and Anne were to consider Lionel—a little. He *is* her husband after all."

Adam took the flowers from her. "Don't interfere

in something you don't understand!" he bit out, his eyes cold and angry. "What have you done with the orchid I gave you instead of a wedding bouquet?"

Her face flushed. "Oh, Adam, how nice of you! But nobody gave it to me! What colour was it?"

"White. I made sure you'd recognise it for what it was, one of the rare Vesak orchids—"

"Oh, Adam, I wish I'd had it!"

"You have flowers enough without."

"I would rather have had yours!"

The muscles tightened in Adam's jaw. "Are you sure you wouldn't rather have had something more lasting from me? Sri Lanka is as famous for her jewels as she is for her flowers."

"But you said the Vesak orchid reminded you of me!" Miranda protested. "That's better than jewels!"

"Don't you believe in the saying that diamonds are a girl's best friend? You must be unique if you don't!"

Miranda strongly resented his imputing Anne's motives to her, but she said nothing.

"I must ask Sita if she's seen my orchid. Someone must have put it somewhere!"

Adam stopped in his tracks. "Don't fuss about it! What's one flower amongst so many?"

Miranda bit back the retort that came to her lips, hiding the hurt he had dealt her as well as she could. But his impatience further undermined her hardly won confidence.

They came to an end of the lines of Estate-workers. Only their priest waited for them to come up to him. He decorated them both with garlands of flowers, twisted together with tinsel more usually found in Europe on Christmas trees. He enveloped them with the smoke of burning incense, uttering sing-song prayers in a language which not even he understood all the while. And he placed little dabs of coloured paste on their foreheads, signifying the god Shiva's acceptance of the worship that was being offered him in their name.

She caught sight of Liam standing uncomfortably a little way off from the group and smiled across the space between them, which Liam returned with a scowl of disapproval.

"What a way for an English girl to be married!" he exclaimed when he finally caught up with her. "Is that supposed to be the Third Eye he's put on your forehead?"

"I shouldn't think so," she said.

His concern etched deep lines into his face. "Look, Miranda, it isn't too late for you to come home with us. I've kept your seat open. If you find you've bitten off more than you can chew, you have only to get in touch and I'll fetch you away somehow. This is no life for you!"

"I have Adam," she reminded him.

"Have you?" He was caustic in his disbelief. "He seems to be more interested in his sister-in-law than you. I notice she's the one who's hanging on his arm now."

Miranda stiffened. "Then I'm free to hang on yours!" she said lightly. "Would you like to escort me back to the house?"

He held out his arm to her without a word. "They call it a bungalow," he murmured when they were more than halfway there. "Another name for a palace in my vocabulary."

Miranda remembered that she had thought exactly the same the first time she had come to Adam's home. She still found it hard to refer to it as a bungalow, but she supposed she would accustom herself to it, as to so much else.

Anne was still beside Adam when he made a speech in Tamil, thanking the workers for their good wishes. Miranda had expected that he would summon her to his side, but he totally ignored her. His eyes rested briefly on Anne's smiling face, almost as if it were she he had married. He didn't even look around for Miranda.

Miranda clenched her fists, trying not to mind such cavalier behaviour. She didn't understand Tamil, she told herself. Yet she could sense that the crowd didn't like Anne Forster any more than she did.

"Let's go inside!" she said to Liam.

"Aren't you expected to be on hand here?"

Miranda's head began to ache. "I've had enough! All I want is to sit down somewhere!"

"If you say so," Liam answered her cheerfully. "You look a bit under the weather."

That was an understatement, Miranda thought, catching sight of herself in the glass in the hall. She was a pale grey colour and her eyes looked unnaturally large in her unhappy face. She tried to pull herself together, to ignore anything that Anne might say or do, but she knew it to be a lost cause. Anne was the one Adam wanted, and she always would be!

She stood in front of the mirror, staring at Adam's mother's wedding-dress. It couldn't have meant anything after all! Yet it was so beautiful! The scarlet shone through the white of the lace, the one enhancing the other, and it suited Miranda as if it had been made for her. She looked almost beautiful, she thought, and was fiercely glad that the dress on Anne would have been a disaster. She hadn't enough colour in herself to carry off such a glowing shade of red, but on Miranda, with her blue-black hair, it lent her a loveliness that she had never seen on herself before.

"I believe there is to be a reception of sorts," she said uncomfortably to Liam. "Some of Adam's friends are coming over for it."

"More speeches!" Liam opined gloomily.

"At least they'll be in a language we can understand!"

"If you ask me, you'd do better to sit down in a comfy chair for a bit, love. I'll leave you on your own in the sitting-room. We can't have you fainting at your own wedding!"

It was nice to be the object of someone's solicitude. Miranda allowed herself to be put in a chair and given a book to read, taken at random from the bookshelves that almost covered one wall of the room.

Anne and Adam came in together a little while later. Miranda didn't have to look at Adam to feel the tension in his powerful body. She thought she knew what had caused that tautness in his muscles too. It had to be Anne, and the closeness of her body to his as she dangled from his arm, looking as if a breath of wind would blow her away.

His grey eyes froze Miranda into immobility. "What are you doing in here, Miranda?" he demanded.

"She felt faint," Liam hurried forward to explain. "I thought it better she should recover quietly by herself."

"With an old friend for company?" Adam drawled dangerously.

"You seemed to be otherwise engaged," Liam pointed out.

Adam's eyes narrowed. "How convenient for you. However, *my bride* seems to be fully recovered now and I am here to look after her. It's time for us to cut the cake, Miranda my dear, if you can tear yourself away from your *friend*."

Miranda jumped to her feet, forgetting the long skirts of her dress, and nearly fell headlong into his arms. She recovered herself, ignoring the hand he put out to help her.

"Isn't Anne coming?" she asked sweetly.

"Of course I'm coming! I wouldn't miss it for worlds!" Anne answered for herself. "Hadn't you better wash your face first, however? Some of our friends are civilised people and they might not understand why you had to submit to that extraordinary ceremony outside just now." She shivered with delicate distaste. "If you'd asked my advice, my dear, I would have told you to leave all such things to Adam. He understands them. The workers always take advantage of anything one tries to do for them. They're a very backward and a not particularly clean people. You should see the state in which they keep their own places! Little better than pig-sties!"

Miranda turned and faced her. "Would we do better if we were as poor as they and had such poverty-stricken shacks to live in?"

"My dear, why give them anything better? If you gave them decent housing, they'd be slums in a couple of weeks."

"What an old, tired argument!" Miranda condemned her fiercely. "People used to say exactly the same about the poor in England. It wasn't worth giving them proper bathrooms because they'd only keep their coal in the bath—"

"Well, they did, didn't they?" Anne said, smoothing her hair with a complacent hand.

"Rubbish!" said Miranda.

Miranda ignored the warning pressure of Adam's hand on her wrist as Anne turned her back on her, still smiling a small, superior smile. She reached out, pulling at the other girl's sleeve. There was a rending sound as Anne's dress gave way, followed by a wail of rage.

"Take that vixen away from me!" Anne cried out to Adam. "It's bad enough having to put up with her here at all, without being attacked by her! You'll have to train her better than that! She may have married you, but she'll never be mistress of what is mine! Tell her that, Adam! Tell her that now!"

Miranda whirled round to face her husband. "Yes, tell me before it's too late to do something about it!" she commanded him.

"I don't have to tell you anything," he retorted.

"I think you do!"

His hands closed on her shoulders, giving her a short, sharp shake. "It's already too late!" he rasped out. "You can't undo what is done! You're married to me and, by God, that's the way you'll stay!"

A mixture of temper and despair lent Miranda a spurious courage. "The marriage is not a marriage yet! I'll have it annulled!"

"Will you?" He spoke the words so softly, she wasn't sure if she had heard them or imagined them. "You're too ambitious, Miranda, if you think you can get the better of me so easily!"

She blanched. "No, Adam. Let me go! We—we have to cut the cake!"

"The cake can wait. You, it seems, cannot!"

He lifted her bodily into his arms, ignoring her entreaties to put her down. "Please, Adam! *Adam!* What will people think?"

"What does it matter what they think?"

"It matters to me!"

"No, Miranda, it does not. All that matters to you is that you please me well enough to make it worth your while to stay—and that is something I am more than capable of doing. Before morning, you will be begging me to allow you to stay! There will be no more talk of bringing our marriage to an end!"

"Not even after you have the child you want?"

He stared into her face, his expression unreadable-to her. "What makes you think I shall ever let you go?" he demanded at last.

"Anne—"

"Anne is not my wife, Miranda. My children will need their mother, as I needed mine. The mothering instinct is the only wholly admirable one which woman is capable—"

"Was that the only reason you loved your mother?"

He lifted her higher still. "Probably." He whirled her round in a circle, bowing ironically at their audience. "I'm sure you'll manage well enough without us, my wife has need of me!"

Miranda's cheeks were scarlet as her face burned with embarrassment. "I'll go with you as soon as the cake is cut!" she pleaded with him, her lips close against his ear.

"Is that another promise you think you can break with impunity if it doesn't suit you when the time comes?" he mocked her.

She shook her head. "Please, Adam."

She found herself on her feet again. "Very well, but I haven't changed my mind, Miranda. The sooner you are my wife in fact the better!"

She felt weak, her bones turned to water. His voice was harsh, but there was a glint in his grey eyes which promised something more, something that set her heart beating frantically against her ribs and which brought a dryness to her mouth. She wished they were already alone together, with no one to see the devastating effect he had on her, no one to witness her weakness where he was concerned.

She tore her eyes away from his face and looked about her. Liam was still scowling, she noticed, and Anne—

Anne was smiling, her eyes too bright for her to be genuinely amused. But it was not at her expression that Miranda was looking. It was at the flower at her breast. A pure white Vesak orchid of the rarest sort. The flower Adam had said he had bought for her, but had obviously given to his mistress.

Chapter Eleven

The cake was cut and Miranda had smiled and smiled until her face ached with the strain.

"Did you give her the orchid?" she accused Adam when she found herself alone with him for a few seconds put together.

"What if I did?"

Miranda went as white as a sheet. "Does she remind you of a particular orchid too?"

He shrugged his shoulders. "Why not? Forget it, Miranda. It's only a flower!"

"Are you sure it's not a symbol of something deeper between you?"

Adam looked fully at her then, the grey of his eyes as cold as ice. "You don't trust me further than you can see me, do you? But you're committed to me all the same now, Miranda!"

"But how committed are you?" she asked him dryly.

"Enough."

"I hope you are. If I'm committed, so are you, and it isn't in my nature to share my husband with another woman. If I stay, Anne goes!"

His expression was as hard as granite. "Is that an ultimatum?"

Miranda swallowed the dry lump in her throat. She hoped she sounded more confident than she felt. "Yes, it is," she said. "I want my orchid!"

"Then ask her for it," Adam suggested smoothly, turning away from her and going to speak with one of his friends who had only just arrived.

It was too much to hope that Anne hadn't noticed how easily Adam had brushed aside her complaint. She came across the room, not bothering to hide her malice. Fingering the orchid, bruising its tender petals, she asked, "Did you think it was for you?" A thin smile curved her lips.

"It's usual for the groom to provide flowers for the matron-of-honour, isn't it?" Miranda answered her.

"But I am more than that!" Anne's compliance was hard to take. "I think my title should be mistress-in-charge, don't you? Mistress of the house *and* of Adam!"

"Until today." Miranda was surprised at the cool, composed sound of her voice. "Now he has a wife of his own. Adam has a very possessive streak in him, or haven't you noticed?"

Anne turned a mottled red, speechless for once.

"Perhaps."

Fortunately, at that moment Liam touched her arm to gain her attention.

Miranda turned to him with relief. They watched Anne make her way through the guests, her ultra-thin body weaving in and out in a way that was curiously reminiscent of a snake.

"Is that the serpent in your Eden?" Liam asked, reflecting her own thoughts.

"I'm jealous of her," Miranda admitted.

"It's not too late to fly home to London with me, remember that! I won't give up hope of you until the very last minute, when they're closing the doors of the aeroplane."

"Oh, Liam," she sighed, "I wish I were in love with you!"

His smile was wry. "What am I supposed to say to that?"

"Goodbye!" Adam's voice said behind them. "Miranda has a date with me!"

"Not yet!" Miranda put in. The sound of his voice did disastrous things to her insides. It destroyed her carefully won independence, but she wasn't going to allow him to know how vulnerable she was. "How are you getting down to Colombo, Liam?"

"We've hired a car to take us." He looked meaningly at her. "We're leaving in the morning at about ten o'clock. We're flying to England tomorrow night."

Miranda's lips trembled. She couldn't bring herself to look at Adam. "I'll be thinking of you," she said.

"You'll have other things to think of by then," Adam told her gruffly. "It's time for us to leave our guests to their own devices, Miranda."

She would have lingered even then, but his fingers closed round her wrist. "Do I have to drag you by the hair?" he asked for her ears only.

"You wouldn't dare!" she challenged him.

"Don't press your luck!"

She glanced at him uncertainly, her eyes as green as emeralds. "I may never see Liam—or the others again," she began to explain.

"One frequently has to give up something on marriage." He dismissed her speech with a marked lack of sympathy.

"What—*whom* are you giving up?"

His fingers touched her cheek, found her chin and turned her face up to his. "I'll let you know if I plan to give up anything," he said with a touch of severity. "Whatever it is, it won't be you!"

"I'll be off then," Liam murmured. "Look after yourself, Miranda!"

She was hardly aware of his going. "Did you give Anne the orchid?" she asked Adam, again.

"You weren't wearing it. I have something else for you."

"I'd rather have had the orchid. It doesn't suit Anne!"

He glanced across the room to where the other woman was standing. Anne turned her head and looked back at him, making a grimace of distaste as she noticed Miranda's flushed face. She excused herself from the portly man she was talking to and came over to Adam.

"Having trouble with your little bride, darling?" she addressed him. "Poor Miranda! You're going to miss your friend, aren't you?"

Adam's hand tightened about her wrist until his grasp was an agony. "Yes," Miranda agreed through clenched teeth.

"She'll manage very nicely without him," Adam said grimly at the same moment. He gave a nod to someone in the party, apparently assenting to something, and a quantity of rice was poured over Miranda's defenceless head.

"How apt!" said Anne. "It is a fertility symbol, isn't it, and that's what she's here for!"

Miranda wondered if she was the only person to have heard her. Adam gave no sign either way. Apparently it was not to be part of his function as her husband to defend her from his mistress. Well, too bad! She would be a slave to no man! She would fight him every inch of the way and she would never surrender!

Miranda lifted her chin. "Adam, I don't want to fight with anyone on our wedding day. We should leave now." There was an insistence in her words that could only make him think she was eager to be alone with him, but she couldn't help that. She had to get away from Anne and her cruel taunts.

Adam put his arms round Miranda and lifted her bodily against his chest. She was afraid she would be too heavy for him, but he showed no signs of strain. On the contrary, he was smiling, as if he had finally achieved something he had been wanting for a long, long time.

It was that thought that brought a pleasing colour into Miranda's face. Another cupful of rice fell on her like a brief shower of rain, stinging her skin and catching in the crevices of her dress. Adam grinned, a triumphant expression in his eyes. It made him look younger, and she realised how seldom she had seen him without that touch of grim cynicism which he seemed to bring to everything.

It was comfortable to be held against the hard wall of his chest and to feel the strong beat of his heart. Her senses swam as he shouldered open the door of his bedroom.

"Adam, I think you ought to know—"

"I've waited long enough!" he responded. He threw her down onto the middle of the bed. "I expect you'd prefer to get out of that gown by yourself? I thought so." Two devils appeared in his eyes. "I wouldn't have allowed anyone else to wear my mother's dress!"

She clenched her fists. "You gave my orchid away!"

"There are other orchids—"

"And other women!"

"Get undressed, Miranda!"

She shook her head. "I'm not going to let you make love to me," she said, her heart thumping. "Not until you get rid of Anne!"

He put one knee on the edge of the bed. "I don't think you're in a position to issue ultimatums. You surrendered your right to do that this afternoon!"

"By marrying you? You made the same vows as I did! Doesn't it bother you to have your mistress under the same roof as your wife?"

"Not a bit."

The audacity of that made her gasp. "Don't you care what anyone thinks?"

"I might care what you think if I didn't know I can

change your mind for you. Take that dress off, Miranda, or I'll tear it off your back myself!"

Her eyes filled with tears. "You'd ruin your mother's wedding-dress without a thought, just as long as you get your own way! Well, you'll have to do more than that before I'll submit to your tyranny!"

"Like the weight of my hand on your backside?"

Miranda sniffed. It was more to prevent the tears from welling over and down her cheeks, but she despised herself for showing any weakness at that moment.

"You're big enough and strong enough, but I've never given in to a bully yet!"

He was disconcerted. "A bully?" he repeated.

"Only a bully would strike a woman!" she pressed home her advantage.

"I haven't struck you yet," he pointed out. "And, if I do, it will be your own fault. Most wives don't have to be coerced into bed by their husbands! Or is this display of nerves merely to underline your innocence in such matters? I seem to remember you expressing some doubts about your performance once before."

Miranda winced away from his cruelty. "If you force me it'll be rape!" she warned him in desperation.

"Will it?" He sounded amused. "You forget I've held you in my arms before and you showed no signs of crying rape then!"

"That was before you gave my orchid to Anne!"

The jealousy in her voice came as a shock to Miranda. He could hardly help knowing how she felt if she went on like that! But it was too late to take the words back and why should he get away with presenting his mistress with his bride's bouquet on his wedding day? Anyone would object to that!

"Women!" he exploded. "Forget Anne! She has nothing to do with you and me!"

"She's living in your house!"

"There are other reasons for that."

"Name one of them!" Miranda invited him. "She isn't even discreet! If she'll tell me what a wonderful time the two of you have been having together these last few days, she'll tell the world!"

"No," he said, "you're the only one she'd tell that. You're the only one who'd believe her."

Miranda sighed. "It doesn't make any difference. Either she goes or I do!"

Adam leaned on the bed, his hand on her chin, forcing her to look at him. The hazel patches in his eyes made her wonder why they ever looked cold and disapproving. They were hot enough to burn her now.

"Neither of you is going anywhere! Make up your mind to it, Miranda, you married me with your eyes open and you're going to have to face up to the consequences sooner or later—"

"Then it'll be later!"

"No, it'll be now." His hand slid behind her back, and the sudden loosening of the bodice of her dress told her he had found the zipper and it would only be a matter of time before he would remove the delicate lace and the scarlet silk petticoat altogether.

"Adam," she protested, "please be careful!"

His mouth found hers and his kiss, which began quite gently, deepened, charging her desire with his own.

"There's no escape for you now!" he said in triumph.

The male scent of him was in her nostrils and her eyes widened as she realised that his after-shave lotion was fresh and his face smooth.

"You've shaved!" she discovered.

A smile tugged at the corner of his mouth. "I thought you'd prefer it."

She giggled suddenly, recovering her nerve. "You smell better than I do! I remind myself of an Indian bazaar!"

He lifted the curtain of her hair, his lips against the soft skin of her neck. "If you promise not to go away I'll give you ten minutes to have a shower and get out of this dress. You looked beautiful in it, sweetheart, but you'll look far more beautiful without it!"

She nodded her head in silence. She knew now that she wouldn't even try to escape. Adam had won again.

"Sita put out my nightdress in the other room. It's a very pretty one," she persuaded him.

"You won't need it!"

She hid her eyes with her lashes, wondering that she should waste time by trying to flirt with him. "Please go and fetch it, Adam."

He bent over her and patted her cheek, allowing his hand to slip down to her breast, covered now only by a single layer of scarlet silk. "I'll be back!"

And there was a distinct threat—or was it a promise?—underlying the words.

She shivered, not entirely in fear. "It would be different if it were a mutual gift," she murmured. "That would be an exchange brought about by—" Her voice faded away as she realised that she could not talk of love to Adam. He had no understanding of what it meant to love anyone. Perhaps, long ago, he had loved his mother, but the gentler side of his nature had long been denied, thanks to his experience with his stepmother and Anne. There had probably been other women too, but none of them had been able to break through the hard shell of cynicism he presented to the world. Why had she ever thought that she would have any better luck than the others?

"I value my freedom too much to make myself a hostage for any woman's whim!" he said abruptly, unconsciously confirming her doubts. "You'll have to be content with sharing my bed."

"On a temporary basis?"

"No, children need both their parents when young. However much you dislike it, here you stay! Don't let wishful thinking mislead you into thinking anything else!"

He was very large, looming over her, and her heart beat painfully.

"Don't you care about *my* freedom?" she forced herself to ask.

"If you were free, would you want anything different from what you have?" he mocked her. "I shan't neglect you, Miranda."

"No, but he wouldn't love her either!" She swung her legs over the edge of the bed, sliding out of his way, clutching the bodice of her wedding dress over her breasts. He took a step towards her and the resulting brush of flesh on flesh produced a *frisson* of excitement that spread slowly through her body, suspending any voluntary motion in her limbs. Adam's eyebrows rose a fraction of an inch and she noticed that he was breathing as heavily as she.

"I'm going to have my shower," she reminded him, making no effort to move.

She felt his hand on the small of her back, whilst the other one eased her hold on her slipping dress. It fell to her feet and she stepped out of it, averting her face from Adam.

"Do you still want me to fetch your nighty?" he asked against her ear.

"Yes!"

He laughed softly, releasing the clasp of her brassière and easing it off her shoulders. "You're beautiful, Miranda. Too beautiful to hide yourself away from your lawfully wedded husband!"

His hands took the place of her fallen clothes, his thumbs gently stroking her nipples. "I've wanted to do this ever since I first set eyes on you! Don't make me wait any longer!"

She had wanted it too. She had a fleeting memory of the golden hairs on his arm as he had held her in front of him on the elephant. She had wanted to run her fingers over the hard muscles that had clasped her so securely and—

"You looked different today in a suit," she said.

"When you were dressed for the procession you looked—like the brigand you are!"

The hazel patches in his eyes almost crowded out the grey. "Is that good or bad?" he teased her.

She put her hands over his, vainly trying to force them away from her body. "I prefer the romantic stranger," she admitted. "You look more at home in a sarong, I mean—"

"You want me to change?" he finished for her on a brief sigh.

"You look very nice," she tried to reassure him, "but I prefer it when—" She stopped, hoping vainly to find the words to finish what she had been going to say. How could she say she preferred him half-naked, as he had been when he had come uninvited to her hotel bedroom? It had pleased her eye to see the ripple of muscles of his neck and chest, and she had found it exciting to feel his warm, tanned skin hard against hers.

"It would seem women are less different from men than I'd supposed," he said dryly. "Can it be you like to look at me too?"

She bent her head, unwilling to acknowledge as much. "I want to take my shower, that's all!"

He let her go with an abruptness that brought home to her how much she wanted to stay where she was. "All right, go and shower, but I'll still be here waiting for you."

The water was only barely warm and restored some of her usual vigour to her body. He had meant what he said, she reflected; he would be waiting for her, and she was fiercely glad that he had effectively cut off her only channel of escape. England had never seemed so far away.

"Miranda Ferguson!" She jumped, sluicing the water onto the tiled floor. Miranda Ferguson? Was that really her? "Miranda, if you don't come out, I'm coming in to get you!"

She wound the only towel she could find around herself and opened the bedroom door. He was standing by the window, as naked as she, with only a length of cloth tied about his middle. On her bed lay the nightdress she had wanted and, in a pile on the floor, were the rest of her clothes, scooped up from wherever he had found them and deposited in the first convenient space he had come across.

"I'm here," she said.

He turned to face her, staring at her as if he had never seen her before. "I brought you your orchid," he said.

She searched the granite contours of his face, wondering if it was anything she had done which had caused the bleak expression. Then her eyes went to the bed where he had placed the orchid on the centre of the pillow.

"Didn't Anne mind?" she heard herself asking.

He shrugged his shoulders. "It wasn't hers to mind about."

"Wasn't it? She was wearing it."

"I shall never give away anything of yours. You ought to know me better than that by now, Miranda. I never give away anything of my own either, and now that you are mine, you may be sure I have no intention of letting you get away from me.

She went past him to the bed and lifted the orchid to her face. It had no scent at 'all, that she could detect.

"Aren't you going to thank me?" His voice was husky and raw with emotion. Was he still angry?

"Not if you wanted to give it to Anne," she said. "I know she means more to you—"

The flower was taken roughly from her hand and tossed onto the floor. Her towel followed, leaving her naked and shaking as she faced him.

"Miranda, don't tease me any more!" he begged her. "I've waited for you all I'm going to wait!"

His chest felt rough against her breasts, but she liked the sensation. She liked it even more when his lips followed the passage of his caressing hands and then returned to her lips, his kisses deepening and insisting on a response that brought her arms up round his neck and arched her body into his.

"Are you ready for love now, sweetheart?"

She didn't answer in words, but her hands sought the knot of his sarong and she loosened it and threw the length of material on the floor to join her towel and the bruised orchid.

"Is it possible, Mrs. Ferguson, that you can want me too?" he asked very gently, pushing her back onto the bed.

It was like a triumphant cry resounding in her ears. He might not love her, not as she wished to be loved and cherished by him, but he had a man's pride in possessing the woman he had chosen. Would he ever love her? And how long would it take him to discover the depth of her love for him?

Her whole body came alive to his touch. His kisses

brought the river of excitement within her into flood, bursting its banks and carrying her into a new world she had never inhabited before, never even suspected was there. Adam was the right man for her. She had no doubt of that. He was everything in a lover she had ever hoped for, firm and masterful, yet with a certain tenderness of which he would have been ashamed in his everyday life.

"Now you're my wife," he said at last.

"Yes, oh yes," she sighed with pleasure. "Yes," she admitted.

He caressed her cheek. "Any regrets, Mrs. Ferguson?"

"No," she breathed. "Have you?"

"Only one. I wish I'd managed to get everything sorted out with Lionel before today. *That* would have made all the difference!"

It certainly would, she thought.

Adam was sleeping. Miranda lay still, listening to his even breathing for a long, long time. If he wanted Anne he could have her! She now knew that she could never bear to share him.

It was easy to slip out of bed without waking him; more difficult to find some suitable clothes to wear from the pile on the floor; more difficult still to pack her belongings in the suitcase she found beneath the pile when she could hardly see anything for the tears in her eyes.

He was still sleeping when Miranda was ready to go. She wanted badly to lean over him and kiss him goodbye, but she contented herself with one last look.

"I love you, Adam Ferguson," she said aloud. "Don't blame me too much."

Her foot brushed against the orchid and she picked it up, putting it in her bag, determined to keep it for the rest of her days. She had to have something of him. She had nothing else, not even a declaration of love to remember him by.

The door opened silently and closed behind her. Miranda stood still in the corridor, hardly daring to breathe, in case the slight sound would wake him. Then, gaining confidence, she walked away from him down the corridor and into the hall. She negotiated the series of steps that led down to the front door. Then she missed a step. A light snapped on a little ahead of her.

It was Anne, fully dressed, with the car keys dangling from her hand. "Had enough of marriage?" Her thin lips curved into a malicious smile.

Miranda tried to push past her.

"I figured you might like a lift to Colombo. It *is* Colombo where you're going to meet your Irish friend, isn't it?" the hateful voice continued. It was more by way of statement than question.

Chapter Twelve

Quite what took Miranda to the church that day she didn't know. She seldom visited it now. She had never noticed the stained glass window before, but she did so now because the main theme in the center was that of the First Death, and there was Adam, the first man, agonising over the dead body of his son and realising what he had lost. To bring the point home, behind him was an angel guarding the closed Gates of Paradise with an outstretched sword.

"Were you hoping I was feeling like that over your loss?"

The familiar arrogant tones froze her to the spot. What was he doing here in Winchelsea?

"Adam?" she whispered.

"Don't you recognise me from my portrait?"

She glanced at the window again. "I prefer the real man," she said.

"You'll forgive me if I demand some proof of that," he said dryly. "You've given little sign of it so far!"

"I thought—" she began.

"You think too much, my love. Women don't usually bother, which is just as well, for they invariably come to the wrong conclusion."

Miranda preferred to say nothing at all. She licked dry lips, hoping for inspiration. "Didn't Anne tell you—"

"What could *she* tell me about you?"

Her heart turned over within her. "I'm sorry," she said.

"Sorry is an easy word to say. Why did you do it, Miranda?"

"You know why I did it!"

"Because you preferred Liam O'Grady after all?"

She was horrified he should think any such thing. *"No!* Oh, Adam, you know I have no particular feeling for Liam!"

"Does *he* know that?" The words fell into a silence and he shrugged his shoulders.

"I've never encouraged Liam!" she protested. "I told him—"

"Told him, Miranda? Told him what? That he'd do nicely as a second string to your bow?"

"I told him—" But Miranda couldn't bring herself to say it. How could she tell this grim-faced Adam what she had told Liam. Adam didn't believe in love! "Adam, what are you doing here?" she asked him instead.

"No wife of mine runs out on me and gets away

with it!" he bit out. "It's freezing in here. Isn't there somewhere else we could go?"

"We could go to my mother's house."

"And have her butting in on us?"

"She isn't there. She's gone to London to visit friends."

He made a gesture for her to lead the way out of the church. "Is this where you would have been married if you'd married O'Grady?"

"I never would have married Liam," she said quietly, closing the door behind them.

"Not man enough for you?" he jeered.

It was no more than the truth. Liam was the brother she had never had, a likable man with likable ways, a man with whom she felt completely at ease, and she might have mistaken that for love if Adam had not come along to break her heart.

"Why did you run away with him?" he said suddenly.

"I wanted you to love me!" It was the last thing she had meant to say and she was appalled at her own lack of self-control.

"What makes you think I didn't?"

She shook her head. "You made love to me. It isn't the same thing."

He was silent, his hands in the pockets of his overcoat. They walked down the street towards her mother's house. She put the key in the lock and opened the door, holding it wide for Adam to follow her.

"I expect you're hungry," she said.

He nodded. "I never eat on aeroplanes. The way

to avoid jet-lag is to drink a lot, not alcohol but anything else. A friend once told me that most of jet-lag is caused by dehydration and it seems to work."

"You should have told me that before!" Miranda said with feeling.

"I didn't know you were going to fly half across the world or I might have," he responded.

"You had Anne," Miranda reminded him.

"I could have wrung her neck—or yours! She might have killed you in that expensive car of hers, or didn't that occur to you?"

"She is a terrible driver," Miranda admitted.

"Then why did you go with her?"

"She was there, and she offered to take me. I would have walked to Kandy if I'd had to, and to get a lift the whole way to Colombo was too good an opportunity to miss."

"Anything to get away from me?"

Miranda shrugged her shoulders in a gesture borrowed from him. "You can't have both of us," she said.

He stood in the middle of the kitchen, dominating the small room in which there was only room for one person to work at best. Idly, he picked up the egg-beater and whirled the blades in mid-air, just as though he had never seen one before.

"What makes you think Anne has anything to do with me?" he asked.

Miranda's mouth fell open. "Everything!" she said comprehensively.

"My brother's wife?" he murmured wryly.

"As if you'd let that stand in your way! Especially

as Lionel seems to let you get away with anything you choose to do! What sort of a man is he to allow his brother to share his wife? It's obvious Anne has no respect for him and I can see why!"

The grimness fell away from Adam like a cloak. "Ah, so you do think a man should have some control over his wife's behavior?"

"Well, yes," Miranda agreed defensively. "I suppose so." She gave him a cautious look, wondering what was coming next.

"I shan't allow O'Grady to take you away from me," he said.

"What if I want to go with him?" Miranda couldn't resist asking.

"You don't. He may be the better man in many ways, but he'll never be able to satisfy you physically as I can. Your body belongs to me even if the rest of you doesn't."

Her face burned. It was humiliating to realise that the memory of her own wantonness was a memory which he would always share. Not even her inexperience had caused her to hold back.

"I've never denied you are physically attractive," she said in a small voice, "and not only to me!"

"Anne has left the bungalow," he told her abruptly.

"What?" She stopped beating, sure she had misheard him.

"Lionel came up from Colombo and took Anne away."

"I thought Lionel was in England?"

"He was. He had to come out to Sri Lanka to sign the papers making the estate over to me. After I'd finished shouting at Anne, I was afraid I might kill her, so I telephoned to him to come and get her. He has more backbone than I'd expected. He told her he's sold the estate to me, that he'd never had any intention of doing anything else because, not only did he hate growing tea, but as an alien he couldn't possibly keep control of the place. Anne tried telling him she was going to stay all the same. She would divorce him and marry me." Adam made a gesture of distaste. "Women get very stupid ideas sometimes. She didn't like it when Lionel pointed out that she was talking about a married man. She said she had taken care of that already."

"She thought she had," Miranda said. "I thought so too."

"So I gathered—from Sita!"

"She doesn't like Anne," Miranda said helplessly.

"No," Adam agreed. He contemplated her shadowed face with narrowed eyes. "Why didn't you tell me what she was up to?"

"But Adam, you knew! It was common knowledge she was staying in your house because she was your mistress."

"She was there because I didn't want her to get wind that Lionel was selling out. She was bound to put a spoke in his wheel if she could. She'd married him for the estate after all, though all she wanted was the money she thought she could wring out of it. Yours is an acquisitive sex, my dear!"

She looked him straight in the face. "Have you found me to be acquisitive?" she challenged him.

In other circumstances the thunderstruck look on his face would have made her laugh.

"You?" he said stupidly.

She touched him on the arm. "Come," she said, "I've something I want to show you."

He followed her obediently up the stairs and she had never realised how narrow they were before. He hadn't seemed so big in his own house, but here, with his overcoat still on, he seemed enormous coming up the stairs behind her.

She led him into the bedroom which had always been hers. "This has been my room all my life," she said simply. "My mother's packed all my possessions in that box ready to send on to me. Have a look and then tell me I'm acquisitive! I haven't anything else in the whole world."

He did as she bade him, his eyes glancing over the few relics of her childhood.

"You're not like other women," he said at last.

"Thank you. From you, I'm sure that's a compliment!"

A reluctant smile tugged at the corners of his mouth. "You've made your point. I guess my view of your sex has been somewhat coloured by two women in particular and you're not in the least like either of them. I wouldn't have wanted to marry you if you had been."

"Anne and your stepmother?"

He nodded. "My mother was different of course, but I couldn't believe that you were too. I didn't want to fall in love with you. I was so afraid you might turn out to be the same. Then I found I couldn't help myself."

Miranda blinked. "You certainly never told me about it! All you wanted from me were children!"

A light came into his eyes. "You should have known better than that, my darling! If I want children, it's because they'll be yours too. I racked my brains for some way of making you stay and that seemed as good a reason as any. I wanted you from the very beginning, more than I'd ever wanted any woman. I thought if I took you to bed once or twice I could get you out of my system, but that didn't appeal to you. Then I realised I wanted you beside me on a permanent basis."

"And didn't you ask yourself why?" Miranda pressed him.

"I didn't want to know the reason why! All I knew was that just when I'd achieved my object and persuaded you to marry me, you ran off with O'Grady."

"I was jealous of Anne," Miranda admitted.

"You had no reason to be. She's been nothing more to me than an irritation for a long time now. Lionel was welcome to her when he married her and, I had long since gotten over my passing infatuation for her. Regardless of what you may think, she has never been more to me than a guest in my house."

Miranda veiled her eyes, afraid he would see the leaping joy in them. "It didn't look that way to me," she said slowly. "You may have wanted to end your affair, but Anne certainly didn't!"

Adam put out his hands to her, pulling her into his arms. "There's never been any woman for me since I saw you, love. There never will be again. I didn't want to tell you so because I was afraid you'd—"

She looked at him then, half-laughing. "Take advantage?"

He nodded. "I was so much in love with you I didn't know what to do!"

"Was?" she queried, her lips trembling into a smile.

He nodded. "I love you," he said. "I love you more than I thought it possible to love a woman. Please come back home with me, Miranda?"

She put her hand on his. "Darling Adam, why do you suppose I married you if it wasn't because I love you more than life itself? I came away because I thought you regretted not waiting for Anne, because I couldn't bear to share you with her. But it broke my heart to leave you—"

"I wanted to tell you the Estate was ours again. Everything I tried to do for you seemed to go wrong! Anne took your orchid out of your room when Sita wasn't looking. Sita was already upset because Anne had turned her out. Perhaps the Estate has always meant more to me than it should, but I thought you'd understand I was sharing with you something that was a part of me. But Lionel hadn't yet signed the papers, and it still wasn't mine to share!"

Miranda reached up and kissed him full on the lips. "Was it so terribly difficult to say you loved me?"

"It comes easier all the time! Nor were you any more open with me, darling! If I'd known you loved me, Liam could have had the run of the house for all I cared. Where is he now, by the way?"

She shook her head at him. "How should I know? I'm not his keeper!"

"Am I yours?" he countered.

"I hope so," she said.

He released himself and sat down on the bed, taking off his overcoat as he did so. "Come here and prove it to me!" he invited her.

But still she hesitated. "You'll never get anything to eat if I do," she warned him.

"It didn't look much of a meal anyway. There are other appetites you are far better equipped to satisfy!"

She laughed. "I won't have aspersions cast on my cooking—" She uttered a shriek of genuine fear as he yanked her off her feet and deposited her on the bed beside him.

Very slowly he began to remove his coat and tie. She began to undress also, shivering against the unheated air in the room. It was warmer held close against him under the blankets, warm and intimate, and her shivering then was of pure pleasure in the feel of his body against hers.

He leaned up on his elbow, tracing the curve of her lips with one finger.

"Love me?" he asked her.

"Yes, please," she said arching her body to his insistent demand. She sighed happily as their lips met in a long kiss. Sita was right, she thought, she knew our love was *written in the stars*.

Silhouette Romance

IT'S YOUR OWN SPECIAL TIME

Contemporary romances for today's women.

Each month, six very special love stories will be yours

from SILHOUETTE.

Look for them wherever books are sold

or order now from the coupon below.

$1.50 each

Silhouette Romance

- - - - - - - - - - - - - - - - -

SILHOUETTE BOOKS, Department SB/1
1230 Avenue of the Americas
New York, NY 10020

Please send me the books I have checked above. I am enclosing
$_____ (please add 50¢ to cover postage and handling. NYS and
NYC residents please add appropriate sales tax). Send check or
money order—no cash or C.O.D.'s please. Allow six weeks for delivery.

NAME_____

ADDRESS_____

CITY_____STATE/ZIP_____

Silhouette Romance

15-Day Free Trial Offer
6 Silhouette Romances

6 Silhouette Romances, free for 15 days! We'll send you 6 new Silhouette Romances to keep for 15 days, absolutely free! If you decide not to keep them, send them back to us. You pay nothing.

Free Home Delivery. But if you enjoy them as much as we think you will, keep them by paying us the retail price of just $1.50 each. We'll pay all shipping and handling charges. You'll then automatically become a member of the Silhouette Book Club, and will receive 6 more new Silhouette Romances every month and a bill for $9.00. That's the same price you'd pay in the store, but you get the convenience of home delivery.

Read every book we publish. The Silhouette Book Club is the way to make sure you'll be able to receive every new romance we publish.

This offer expires January 31, 1982

Silhouette Book Club, Dept. **SBF17B**
120 Brighton Road, Clifton, NJ 07012

Please send me 6 Silhouette Romances to keep for 15 days, absolutely free. I understand I am not obligated to join the Silhouette Book Club unless I decide to keep them.

NAME_____

ADDRESS_____

CITY_____ STATE_____ ZIP_____

READERS' COMMENTS ON SILHOUETTE ROMANCES:

"Your books are written with so much feeling and quality that they make you feel as if you are part of the story."

—D.C.*, Piedmont, SC

"I'm very particular about the types of romances I read; yours more than fill my thirst for reading."

—C.D., Oxford, MI

"I hope Silhouette novels stay around for many years to come. . . . Keep up the good work."

—P.C., Frederick, MD

"What a relief to be able to escape in a well-written romantic story."

—E.N.. Santa Maria, CA

"Silhouette Romances . . . Fantastic!"

—M.D., Bell, CA

"I'm pleased to be adding your books to my collection—my library is growing in size every day."

—B.L., La Crescenta, CA

* Names available on request.